"Ow! Don't put your knee there," Murdock growled from somewhere beneath her

"Oh, good heavens!" Georgie groaned in mortification. "I'm so sorry."

Wriggling and twisting, she floundered helplessly on top of him. Her head was jammed under the arm of his leather jacket, her cheek pressed against his shirt. With one hand pinned beneath her side, the other draped over his chest and her legs sticking straight out of the box, she struggled to find her way out.

"That's my face you've got your elbow in," he grunted. "And stop squirming like that."

"I'm trying to get out. What's wrong with you? Do you want to stay here all night?"

"If you keep wiggling like that I do."

Reaching for the battered edge of the box, his words brought her up short. Surely she hadn't heard him right? When her head snapped up, she caught the quick gleam of a slow, wolfish grin. Her heart skipped a beat. Oh, sweet Lord, Georgie thought in sudden realization.

That wasn't a gun pressed against her stomach!

Kathy Marks thoroughly enjoys writing about the craziness of love. "In a lot of ways, falling in love is like intensive trauma. It's devastating, earth-shattering and one of life's greatest sources of amusement," she says. "Nobody acts goofier than a man and woman on the brink of all-consuming passion." In *The Littlest Detective,* Kathy's first Temptation novel, life is about to take one of its wackier twists for two lonely private eyes who have no idea that their lives are going to be changed forever.

Kathy lives with her husband and her two almost-human mutts, Dugan and Murdock, in Tempe, Arizona.

Books by Kathy Marks

YOURS TRULY
18—SEDUCING SYDNEY

SUPERROMANCE
WRITING AS CATHERINE JUDD
587—DANCE OF DECEPTION
603—INDISCREET

THE LITTLEST DETECTIVE
Kathy Marks

Harlequin Books

TORONTO • NEW YORK • LONDON
AMSTERDAM • PARIS • SYDNEY • HAMBURG
STOCKHOLM • ATHENS • TOKYO • MILAN
MADRID • WARSAW • BUDAPEST • AUCKLAND

For Connie Flynn Alexander and
Laurie Schnebley Campbell,
my beacons in the night

ISBN 0-373-25696-5

THE LITTLEST DETECTIVE

1

Love and murder will out.
—William Congreve

ON A BLUSTERY APRIL night in Chicago, Georgina Poulopoulos—who everyone but her late aunt Euphemia called Georgie—slumped behind the wheel of her Volkswagen in a deserted residential street and tried to recapture her earlier enthusiasm for detective work. It wasn't easy.

Flicking on the radio, she scanned the stations for a peppy tune, then turned it off in disgust. She moved her seat forward an inch, then back two. Next she tried stretching her legs across the passenger seat, leaning her head against the side window and reading *Psychologic Profile of a Serial Killer* by the glow of the streetlight.

It was no use. She slammed the book closed. Her first real case for Poulopoulos Investigations, Inc., Georgie admitted, was a bore.

She peered at her wristwatch. Only fifteen minutes had passed. Three and a half hours until Uncle Nikos sent someone to relieve her. A virtual eternity.

Georgie glanced up at the lighted apartment, and made a face at it. Jimmy Ray Thompson wasn't going anywhere tonight. She didn't have to be Jane Marple to realize that he was probably tucked up in bed with the late-night movie still playing . . . while she was out here in the dark, windswept street—cold, sleepy, bored witless, and with an increasingly insistent urge to use a rest room.

Heaving a melodramatic sigh, Georgie fished in her oversize purse for a bag of potato chips and munched a few to stave off the vague gnawing in her stomach. Nerves, she told herself.

Nibbling slowly to make the bag last longer, she leaned her head back, keeping one eye on the apartment window, and thought about Howard Kavin, the hollow-cheeked middle-aged man with the large, sad eyes who'd wrung his hands in her uncle's office and begged them to help him save his daughter from Jimmy Ray. His life, he'd said, depended on it.

Georgie had felt real sympathy for his anguish. Still, she reasoned, even a life-and-death case couldn't deter the inevitable call of nature indefinitely. Despite taking tiny bites, she finished off the last potato chip and wiggled uncomfortably. She swiveled to look through the rear window, and gazed longingly at the bright sign of the diner two blocks away, then eyed with distaste the wide-mouthed plastic jar her uncle's secretary had handed her.

No way was she going to use that jar in place of a ladies' room, surveillance or no surveillance. Dedication had to stop somewhere. With just the tiniest twinge of guilt, George shot a final glance at the apartment window, opened her door and stepped into the drizzling rain.

Five minutes later and feeling much more pleased with the world, she hurried back toward her car. The wind had picked up and she walked quickly with her head lowered. That was how she nearly missed it. Just as she passed a dark blue Buick parked three cars from hers, she caught a fleeting but unmistakable glimmer of movement behind its tinted windows.

Georgie's heart gave an involuntary, sickening thud. For just a moment she froze, caught in the paralyzing grip of panic. Then she was running. Yanking open the door to her car, she dived in, slammed home the lock and ducked out of sight. Breathlessly she lay across the front seat, her mind racing.

Someone was in that Buick! But how? The dented and battered old car, big as a boat, had been parked along the curb at eleven o'clock when she'd first pulled up, she remembered. But ever since she'd been sitting in front of Jimmy Ray's apartment, she hadn't seen a single person approach it.

Which meant, Georgie thought with alarm, who-ever was in that car had been sitting there the whole time she'd been on surveillance. A cold sweat broke out on her forehead at the thought.

Despite the almost irresistible urge to start her own car and speed away, Georgie finally forced herself to scoot up and peer through the rear window. A loud crunch filled the silence, making her jump. Impatiently she swept away the crumpled potato-chip package, then cautiously peeked over the top of the headrest. Sure enough, she saw another quick, furtive flash of light.

Gaping at the dark car in disbelief, Georgie briefly wondered if she might be imagining things. Then she noticed the driver's door inch open a fraction.

With widening eyes she watched as the silhouette of a tall, well-built man in a hat slowly emerged and stood quietly in the rain beside the open door, surveying the empty street. When he took a step away from his car, Georgie's mouth went dry.

"Oh, my God," she gasped, hiding behind her seat again. Squeezing her eyes shut, she raised a shaking hand to her mouth.

In that moment of panic, a whole series of dreadful scenarios played through her head. She'd been followed. Someone had tailed her to the apartment. Someone was watching her, just as she was watching Jimmy Ray Thompson. She was going to be killed, shot down in cold blood on her very first case.

Good heavens! If she wasn't murdered, Uncle Nikos was going to send her back to filing old reports or, worse, fire her. No! No, she'd rather just be shot dead and get it over with.

A dark shadow flitted past the car window, arresting her litany of doom. This was it, she thought. She had to brace herself for death, no matter how slow and agonizing.

With her heart pounding, Georgie listened for the approach of stealthy footsteps. After several silent minutes of breathless waiting, she finally realized that the man hadn't stopped at her car. Instead, he'd passed by and had disappeared down the street.

Surprise and chagrin made her sit up. The dark, rain-slick street was empty. In puzzlement, Georgie gnawed on the tip of her thumb, then went still. There *had* been a man in that car. So, where had he gone? And what had he been doing?

As though in answer, the light in the apartment across the street went out, leaving the face of the building in total darkness. Jimmy Ray Thompson, Georgie thought with sudden inspiration. Whoever was in the Buick might have been watching the young man, too. From what she'd heard of Jimmy Ray, he could easily have any number of people after him.

As Georgie considered all the possibilities—from enraged fathers to hired hit men—a tall phantomlike figure broke away from the darkness of the buildings half a block away. The large man from the Buick, his features hidden in shadow, emerged from the black mouth of an alley, his long overcoat billowing behind him. Astonished, Georgie saw that he was fumbling with the zipper on his pants.

An involuntary smile twitched at the corners of her mouth, even as she slithered into hiding once more. This time—reassured by his not having gunned her down earlier—she peeped out the back window and saw him reenter his car.

Georgie frowned and chewed her thumb again. Now what was she going to do? How could she find out who he was? And more importantly, how was she going to discover *what* he was doing here?

Because, of course, she had to find out. No private detective worth her weight in beans would just sit and do nothing. She drummed her fingers on the steering wheel. To walk into Uncle Nikos's office tomorrow and say "Someone else is watching Jimmy Ray, but I have no idea who he is" was unthinkable. She'd be back filing reports faster than she could say "Sherlock Holmes." The problem was, she couldn't think of a solitary tactic for finding out what the man in the Buick was up to . . . short of walking straight up to his car and asking him.

Georgie paused, the tattoo of her fingers on the steering wheel abruptly stilled. Well, why not? It could work. It could also get her into a bundle of trouble, her more sensible half reminded.

Peeping over the headrest at the dark Buick, Georgie's curiosity grew, tormenting her like an itch she couldn't scratch, until finally she sat upright and took a deep, fortifying breath. Would Sam Spade sit quaking in *his* car? she chastised herself. Hadn't she worked her way through eight years of night classes at college, studying the psychological workings of the criminal mind, for just such a moment?

Quickly, before she had time to reconsider, Georgie made herself throw open her door and step into the street. A gust of raw, damp wind blew down on her, instantly chilling her to the bone and snatching at her heavy trench coat. Her hair blew across her face in a thick, dark veil, and she stumbled as she brushed it from her eyes.

Establish a rapport, she repeated to herself encouragingly as she walked rapidly toward the Buick. Be pleasant and cheerful, and gain his trust. Criminals respond well to positive interactions, she knew from one of her psychology classes. Even cold-blooded, psychotic killers can display rational, appropriate behavior...given time and plenty of Thorazine therapy.

She was nearly at the car now, its windows so dark and streaked with rain that the man inside was hidden. For just a moment she wavered, then steeled herself. Rapping on the window with her knuckles, she cupped her hands to peer inside.

With a gasp of horror, Georgie froze. The barrel of a gun stared back at her, a mere quarter-inch of glass separating that deadly steel eye from the tip of her nose.

She felt the blood drain from her face and the hair on the back of her neck stand up. She wanted to back away. She wanted to close her eyes, fixed now on that lethal little hole, and to lower her hands, but her body refused to obey.

Terror-stricken, she watched the window slowly move down. She saw the crown of a hat first, the soft felt dark with rain and worn shiny with wear. The rim of the hat was dented and misshapen, and it cast a dark shadow across the deep-set eyes that next appeared. The window lowered still farther, and an arrogant, aquiline nose that might have looked noble before it had been broken was visible beneath the shadow of the hat. The nose was flanked by high, chiseled cheekbones like slabs of granite and offset by a square, rugged jaw, rough-hewn and covered in stubble.

It was a hard, weathered face, unrelenting and as tough as iron. The face of a man who'd seen plenty in his three or four decades of life. Only the mouth showed any trace of softness. Full and sensual, his lips hinted at gentler passions, and Georgie felt a small twinge of hope. Then he smiled.

A row of strong, white teeth slowly appeared, bared in a dangerous, wolfish grin. Georgie heard herself give an involuntary gasp. Mesmerized by that intimidating smile, she could only gape at the man.

The gun he held just before her nose never wavered, and Georgie racked her brain for something, *anything* to say to calm him down. At last she looked straight into his eyes, hidden in shadow, and gave him a weak, uncertain smile. "Um . . . hi there."

He didn't twitch a muscle.

Georgie's smile faltered and she bobbed her head in a series of nervous nods.

"Nice car," she said inanely, patting the rusted door gingerly. "Very nice."

She thought she saw his eyes narrow.

"Yes, well." She gave a quick, brittle laugh. "I think I'll just be on my way now. If that's all right with you."

He was as silent as stone. Latent aggression, she concluded. Glancing at the gun, she decided that perhaps "latent" wasn't exactly accurate.

She cleared her throat nervously. "So, I'll just…just leave you now to, uh, go about your… your whatever you're going about. Yes, well, I… It's been nice talking with you. Very nice. I have to go now. That's all right with you, isn't it? I mean, I hope it's okay because that *is* a gun you're holding. You know that, don't you? A gun."

He moved so quickly, twisting his hand and pointing the muzzle up and away from her, that Georgie gave a strangled gurgle of fear. She stared at the man, openmouthed.

"Who are you?" he asked gruffly, his voice low and deep like thunder in the mountains.

Georgie swallowed hard. "Me?"

"What do you want?" he demanded. "Come on. Spit it out. I already spotted you earlier."

"I… I," Georgie sputtered. She glanced warily at the gun, then frowned at him. "What about you? Who are you?"

If anyone could look fierce and astonished at the same time, this man did. Without moving a hair, he managed to convey surprise and something else.

Annoyance, Georgie guessed.

"I asked you to explain," he repeated, his gravelly voice a bit menacing. "I asked you first."

"Well…" Georgie scraped the toe of her shoe against the wet pavement. "Well, I wanted to *know* first. What are you up to?"

She thought that sounded all right. Like a professional, experienced, confident detective…one with backup. She hoped he thought so, too.

The man watched her in silence for nearly a full minute. Just when Georgie began to grow nervous again, he raised the hand that held the gun and pushed the brim of his hat up with the muzzle, revealing intelligent gray eyes, as cool as blue steel.

Apprehensively, Georgie watched as he reached into the inner pocket of his overcoat. When he pulled out a thin leather wallet and flipped it open to reveal the identification of a private investigator, her expression was blank with surprise. She caught a glimpse of his picture and the Illinois crest, but she didn't have time to read his name before he snapped the case shut.

"All right, lady? Satisfied?"

"But—"

"Take a little advice, huh? Don't be so nosy. Next time you might stick that pretty face of yours up to the wrong window."

"You're a P.I.?"

"That's what it says. Now, run along home," he said. With a dismissive shrug, he started to roll up the window.

"Stop!" Georgie grabbed for the edge of the window. "I want to talk to you. I want to—"

"Lady," he said, his words a growl of exasperation. "Go away."

"Wait a minute. Just hold on a second." Fumbling in the back pocket of her jeans, Georgie pulled out the temporary identification Uncle Nikos had made up for her, promptly dropping it in a puddle in her haste.

"Just wait a minute," she repeated, and bent down to scoop it up. She shook off muddy water, and showed him her ID, presenting it to him with just the slightest and most modest of flourishes.

For the second time that night, Georgie thought she saw a shadow of surprise cross his face. He looked at the identification, then at her, then back to her picture. Suddenly, his lips twitched and he gave her another of his slow, wicked smiles.

"Good God," he pronounced slowly. "What is this profession coming to?"

"Very funny," Georgie retorted, wiping rain from her face. "I think you can see now why we need to talk."

"No, lady. I don't see." He began once more to roll up his window. "Now, beat it."

In desperation, Georgie flung herself at the glass. "Are you watching Jimmy Ray Thompson? Are you? Who's paying you to watch him?"

The words were barely out of her mouth, when he turned and fixed her with a stare. She watched as his eyes grew as cold and icy as the gray waters of Lake Michigan in January.

"What do you know about old Jimmy Ray?" he asked, his voice deadly quiet.

"I knew it!" Georgie smacked the side of the Buick and winced. "I knew it. You *are* tailing him. Damn it, you can't. He's my pigeon. This is my case."

"Your *pigeon?* Where'd you learn to talk like that? You sound like an old B-movie."

"It's my case," Georgie repeated. "And you're getting in the way."

"Oh, for God's sake," he grumbled. "*Your* case? What're you talking about? Look at you. Barely out of diapers. Besides which," he added, managing to sound even more scornful, "you're a woman."

Georgie shook her damp hair off her face and straightened her shoulders in preparation to do battle. If there was one thing she couldn't stand, it was a male chauvinist. "Flattery will get you nowhere. What, may I ask, does my gender have to do with anything?"

He grabbed at his hat and yanked it off, revealing a thatch of hair like a wheat field—thick, golden-brown and unevenly mown. Glaring at her, he nearly leaned out the window to shove his face close to hers.

"Look, lady, I don't have time to chat. All right? So buzz off. Blow your own cover if you want. But don't blow mine. Standing out there, hollering like a banshee. My God, the day they let women into the—"

As though struck by a fist, he suddenly went completely, unnervingly still. Georgie frowned at him in bewilderment, then narrowed her eyes.

"Excuse me? Hello? You were saying something about women," she prompted haughtily. "Please, finish. I'm very interested. Believe me, I'm just dying to hear what—"

"Shut up!" he hissed with unexpected violence. Throwing open his door, he knocked her cleanly off her feet.

In disbelief Georgie felt herself begin to fall. Blindly, wildly, she flailed her arms and tensed her muscles for impact. But before she hit the pavement, a huge hand grabbed her shirtfront. Another took hold of the back of her trench coat, and before she knew what was happening, she was hauled unceremoniously into the front seat of the Buick.

For a long, stunned moment Georgie lay on the seat, gasping like a landed fish. She smelled coffee, the mustiness of wet wool and something faintly pleasant and clean. Cologne. Then she realized that the cold metal square against her cheek was his belt buckle.

"Oh, sweet heaven," she began, raising her head from his lap and banging it on the steering wheel. Tears of pain came to her eyes. "How *dare* you? You can't do this. I'll scream. I swear I'll scream so loud the whole neighborhood will hear me. You won't get away with—"

"Would you pipe down? And stay low."

"Low?" Georgie sat up, rubbing the back of her head and reaching behind her for the door handle. "You're in trouble, mister. You'll never get away with this. I'm a black belt in karate. This is no passive victim you've picked, believe me. And when my uncle finds out, he'll make sure you never work again. He'll have your license revoked faster than you can—"

"Don't you ever shut up?" Turning from the window, he scowled blackly at her. "Did you want to be seen?"

"Seen?"

"Our mutual friend is on the move."

"Our mutual...? Our what?" Georgie's eyes widened, and she spun in the seat to stare out the windshield. "He is? Where? Where is he?"

The man raised a large, work-roughened hand and pointed. "There. Just going past the trash cans."

Georgie clutched the dashboard. "My word. He is. That's Jimmy Ray." She paused and gave the stony-faced man beside her an expectant look. "Well, come on."

He blinked at her. "What?"

With a roll of her eyes, Georgie let out a groan of agitated impatience. "Come on, come on. Don't just sit there. Go after him."

"I'm going to. Just as soon as you get out of my car."

Georgie tugged at the dash, nearly bouncing on the seat with urgency. "Hurry up!"

"Get *out*."

"Come on! He's getting away."

"Lady, I don't know who the hell you are."

"What does that matter?" Georgie practically screeched. "You're going to lose him."

The man stared at her, his face a study of suspicion and indecision. He glanced down the street at the rapidly retreating figure, then pushed the key into the ignition with a vicious twist. "I don't believe this."

"He's turning the corner. Come on, come on. Hurry up."

"All right!" he snarled.

At the street corner, they pulled to the curb and watched Jimmy Ray Thompson amble, loose-limbed and carefree, down the side street to a row of padlocked garage doors.

"Okay. Get out now," the man said.

Georgie folded her arms and refused to look at him.

"Lady, I'm warning you. Get out of my car."

"No way," Georgie retorted. "This is my case."

"Lady—"

"Forget it."

Just then, a silver Porsche sprang from one of the garages. With an infuriated glare, the man pulled out after it. "Of all the damned luck," he grumbled under his breath.

"Where do you think he's going?" Georgie grabbed a small notebook from her purse and recorded the license number and the time.

The man beside her hunched grumpily over the steering wheel, cross as an old bear, and didn't answer. In silence they turned out of the residential area and onto a main artery.

"Maybe he's meeting someone," Georgie murmured hopefully. "I'll bet he's meeting another woman."

The surly man driving shot her a disbelieving look. "What?" He shook his head in derision.

Georgie frowned at his tone. In the passing lights of the street, the craggy planes and angles of his face were stark and defined, as though he'd been cast in marble and each line exaggerated. Georgie suddenly realized that he was handsome. Even with the three-day beard, his profile was striking in its rugged masculinity.

"You know what? I didn't catch your name back there," Georgie said as they followed the Porsche onto another side street.

He ignored her.

"I'm Georgie. Georgie Poulopoulos."

Concentrating on the Porsche ahead, his glance at her was swift and dark. She gave him a bright, winsome smile, and his scowl deepened. Yet the next instant he seemed to relent a little.

"Murdock," he barked simply.

"Murdock," Georgie repeated and waited. "That's it?"

"Yep."

"Don't you have a first name? You must have another. Everyone has a Christian name. Sometimes two or even—"

"Just Murdock."

"Murdock." Georgie studied him closely. "You don't like talking much, do you, Murdock?"

"Nope."

He turned a corner then slowed the car to a crawl as they crept past a dimly lit nightclub. Jimmy Ray's Porsche was parked at the curb and the front door was still swinging shut behind him. Slipping the Buick into a parking spot across the street, Murdock reached for his door handle at the same time Georgie reached for hers.

"No," he ordered in a voice that brooked no argument. He pointed his finger at her. "You stay put."

"What? You've got to be kidding. I'm going in there with—"

"You stay out here."

Something hard in his face made Georgie release her door handle. Seething with frustration, she watched him cram his hat back onto his head and climb out. He crossed the street, moving quickly. Pushing past a crowd of miniskirted women and men in leather jackets, he disappeared into the club.

Georgie glanced at her watch, trying to be patient. But in the end, curiosity won out. She barely gave him a full minute before she slipped from the car and followed in his footsteps.

THE CLUB WAS NOISY and crowded, the air hot and smelling of sweat and cheap perfume. At the far end under flashing colored lights, a crush of dancers churned and seethed on the little dance floor. Georgie's stomach did a sick flip-flop at the reeking clouds of cigarette smoke.

Ignoring her queasy stomach, she stood on tiptoe to peer through the throng and spotted Jimmy Ray at the far end of the room, leaning a skinny elbow on the bar and laughing with a tall bartender whose face was so chalky-white he looked like a corpse. Murdock sat hunched on a stool a safe distance away, his hat on the polished wood before him and the heel of one scuffed cowboy boot hooked over the chair rail. As she watched, a short, stocky bartender deposited a drink in front of him.

Nervously, Georgie wiped her palms on her jeans, took a deep breath and advanced.

"Darling!" she cried, swinging prettily onto the stool beside Murdock and turning so she could watch Jimmy Ray. "I'm so sorry I was late. We got held up at the office again. You know how hectic work has been... What? Oh, yes, thanks. I'll have a... a, well, whatever he's having."

Ignoring Murdock's stupefied stare, she wrapped her hand around his arm and laid her cheek playfully on his shoulder. Muscles as hard as steel bands jumped at her touch.

"Have you been waiting long?" she asked sweetly, and gave him her most engaging smile.

His look was black and dangerous. "What are you doing in here?"

Georgie shrugged with what she hoped was nonchalance. "Just doing my job. That's all. Just doing my job."

"I told you to—"

"Wow," Georgie breathed, her eyes focused on the other end of the bar. "No! Don't look. The bartender's handing Jimmy Ray something. Money, I think. He's putting it in his—"

"That's six bucks for both of 'em," the other bartender said, setting down a glass of pale amber liquid in front of Georgie.

Raising her eyebrows expectantly, Georgie smiled at Murdock and was rewarded with a look of grim obstinacy. When she continued to gaze patiently up at him, he let out a series of short, unintelligible grunts, finally pulled out his wallet and slapped the money on the bar.

"How nice of you, sweetheart," Georgie said brightly, and raised the glass to her lips. "Cheers."

Despite her show of sophistication, the sip she took was experimentally small. Nevertheless, the instant she swallowed, her breath left her lungs in a painful gasp. Red-hot lava burned a stinging trail down her throat, bringing tears to her eyes and making her nose run. Throughout her long coughing fit, Murdock merely gazed disinterestedly at her, never batting an eyelash.

"Ahh. Ugh. That's horrible," Georgie choked out when she could finally breathe again. "What is this stuff?"

He shook his head in resigned disbelief and turned away from her to glance down the bar. With a tall, strawberry-pink drink in his hand, Jimmy Ray Thompson looked as if he was settling in for a long chat with the cadaverous bartender.

"Do you drink this on a regular basis?" Georgie asked, raising her glass and examining it with distaste. "No wonder you've got such a negatively emoted personality."

"I've got a what?"

Before Georgie could reply, she felt a hard tap on her shoulder. Swiveling on her stool, she found herself staring at a leather-clad torso. Slowly she looked up and into a pair of small, pink-rimmed eyes set too close together in a face scarred with acne. The man wore a silver stud in one nostril, and a thin gold ring pierced his upper lip. Clearly, Georgie thought in a panic, this was a person with antisocial tendencies.

"Wanna dance?"

Georgie gaped up at him, too unnerved to answer.

"I said, you wanna dance?"

He'd probably never received any positive feedback as a child, Georgie told herself, and tried to warm † him. But her voice still came out like a frightened squeak.

"Dance?" She gulped.

"Yeah. What's wrong with you? You deaf? Let's go."

Appalled, Georgie felt Pierced Lip reach for her arm. But before he could yank her from her stool, a low, barely audible voice rumbled from somewhere behind her, "She's with me."

2

As though this was what he'd been waiting for, the leather-jacketed man froze. Then his lips stretched back in a smile, revealing gray-green teeth. He took a step toward Murdock, his bloodshot eyes hardening with aggression.

"I don't think I heard you right," he taunted. "What'd you say, fella?"

Wide-eyed, Georgie looked back at Murdock. He was huddled over his drink, his eyes on the glass he gripped in his hand, his expression inscrutable.

"I said," Murdock repeated quietly, "she's with me."

"Oh, yeah?" Pierced Lip sneered. "Is that so? She got your name on her somewhere? Hey, honey, stand up and show me where he put his name on you."

A few of Pierced Lip's buddies had gathered closer, and they guffawed at this stunning show of wit. Georgie saw Murdock sigh quietly. He looked with regret at his drink. Briefly he closed his eyes. Then he pushed back his stool.

It seemed to take a long time for him to stand completely upright. Georgie was willing to bet it felt that way to Pierced Lip, as well. Very slowly Murdock rose to his feet, and he seemed to grow taller and broader, until he towered over Pierced Lip and his friends. Unhurried, almost with bored weariness, he crossed his muscled arms over his chest and gazed coolly down at the man.

The sneer on Pierced Lip's face faded, and he wet his thin lips as he took a small, almost imperceptible step backward.

"Hey," he said, raising his hands palms up. "What's the problem? I was just kidding around. That's all."

Silently Murdock watched him, his eyes expressionless.

"I don't even *like* this song," the man continued in a conciliatory tone. "So, no hard feelings, huh? What d'ya say?"

Murdock narrowed his eyes, and the man gave a nervous laugh.

"Cool. All right. We're all friends here. You're a lucky man, dude," he said, taking another backward step. "Real lucky. Got yourself a fine-lookin' woman."

Georgie was aware of a sudden tensing of Murdock's body. Pierced Lip must have sensed it, too, because he backed away more quickly, then suddenly turned tail and disappeared into the crowd.

Sighing, Georgie slumped on her stool in relief. The next instant, her eyes flew open in surprise.

"Outside," she heard a voice growl as a large, solid hand hauled her off her stool and propelled her rapidly through the bar and out the front door.

On the sidewalk, Murdock glared down at her with a murderous look. She waited for the barrage of words, but he only dropped her arm, spun on his heel and headed for the Buick.

"Wait," Georgie cried, flying after him. "Wait! What about Jimmy Ray? Murdock, hold up a minute. Where are you going?"

She caught up to him at the car and clung to his arm.

"Jimmy Ray," he said with quiet, simmering anger, "is gone."

"Gone? Gone where?" She watched him get into the car. "Wait! Where are you going?"

Slamming his door—with unnecessary force, Georgie thought—he started the engine and she suddenly realized she was going to be left behind if she didn't get a move on. Racing around to the passenger door, she yanked it open just before he locked her out. Quickly, she slid onto the seat.

"I'm sorry," she said, gathering her trench coat around her. "I'm sorry about that scene back there. But surely you can't blame me. It wasn't my fault that—"

The look he shot her was dark and deadly and effectively stopped any other argument she might have made. In uncomfortable, smoldering silence, they drove back to Jimmy Ray Thompson's apartment. Jimmy Ray was just walking into the building as they cruised slowly past.

"He's here," Georgie exclaimed happily, and turned in her seat. "It's all right then, Murdock. No harm's been done. We didn't lose him."

Murdock pulled the car next to the curb and stomped on the brakes.

"Out," he barked.

"But—"

"*Get out of my car.*"

Georgie stared helplessly at the hard, craggy face he turned away from her. Meekly, more miserable than she could ever have explained, she reached for the door. As she pushed it open, she glanced once more at his rigid profile.

"Murdock, I—"

"Beat it."

Georgie sighed and bit her bottom lip. "All right," she murmured. "I'm going. I just wanted to say, well, thanks for rescuing me."

Although she waited, he didn't give any indication that he'd heard her. After a moment, she stepped onto the pavement, shutting the door behind her.

MURDOCK TOSSED his canvas rucksack on the scarred, narrow bar and sank wearily onto a stool. In a corner booth by the jukebox slouched Lucky Lutz, who hadn't been lucky at the track since the day they banned him from the stables. He was asleep, his head on the Formica-topped table, a beer bottle still clutched in his hand.

The little tavern was quiet this early in the morning. Tiny dust motes danced in the few brave rays of sunlight that managed to slip through the grime on the windows, and the place reeked of fried food and stale beer. Above the bar, the TV was tuned to a morning talk show, where a sleekly groomed host and hostess flashed expensive megawhite smiles and chatted vivaciously with a group of scared-looking women in new clothes and too much makeup.

Eddie, the owner, stood slump-shouldered behind the bar, watching the program. He waited for the commercial before turning and acknowledging Murdock, who he had, of course, known was there all along.

"Coffee?"

Murdock nodded and rubbed his eyes. His lids felt like sandpaper.

"Want some breakfast?" Eddie asked, setting the mug on the bar.

Murdock thought of the gummy accumulation of grease in the squalid, dark hole Eddie had the audacity to call a kitchen. He shook his head. "Just coffee."

"You gotta eat," Eddie said. When that got no reply, he asked, "So, you been out all night?"

Again Murdock nodded. He wiped the rim of the cup with his thumb, just to be on the safe side, then took a scalding mouthful. The coffee was bitter and practically thick enough to stand a spoon in, but it was hot and strong and Murdock felt life stir in his tired body.

"Guess you got the case wrapped up then?" Eddie went on, leaning conversationally on the bar.

"No. Just stopped by for a shower and a change of clothes."

Eddie glanced over his shoulder at the TV. The grinning couple had returned. Picking up a remote control from the bar, he changed the channel to a wrestling match. Then he turned back and looked hard at Murdock.

"Why don't you get yourself a couple assistants?" he asked at last. "And don't tell me you can't afford it. You could afford a lot better than any of this." He waved an arm vaguely around the bar. "You been raking in the big bucks for years. But what do you ever do with it? You're going to kill yourself, Murdock, working these kinds of hours, year after year—"

Murdock set his mug firmly on the bar. "What's Lucky doing in here?"

Eddie paused, then shrugged. "Irene threw him out again. Claimed he put the money for the electricity bill on the fifth race. He denies it, naturally."

"Naturally."

Eddie studied him, then leaned closer. "Listen, I'm not kidding. You're only thirty-five. You're a young man still. But you won't live to see forty if you keep up this way. A successful man should know how to enjoy his success and to make something of what he—"

"Who says I'm successful?" Murdock demanded defensively.

Eddie scoffed. "Don't give me that. You're the best P.I. this city's ever seen. Everyone knows that. Hell, you're always turning down cases. You could have a dozen people working under you and still not keep up with business."

"What do I need more business for? Anyway, I have Reilly. He's all the help I need."

"Rummy Reilly? Please, don't make me laugh. I'm talking *real* employees. Investigators. But no, you've got to go it alone. Do it the hard way. You deny yourself every creature comfort. Even the luxury of sleeping in your own bed for one full night. You can't keep beating yourself up, day after day, for something that happened years ago. Something you couldn't have prevented if you—"

With a loud scrape, Murdock pushed back his stool and reached for his rucksack. "I gotta take a shower," he said gruffly, and stood up.

"That's right," Eddie snapped, his color rising. "Go take a shower. Then hit the trail again. Go ahead and work your sorry, miserable butt into an early grave. What do I care? I'm just your damned friend."

"Not," Murdock said quietly, "because anyone asked you to be."

Before Eddie could respond, Murdock turned and strode toward the back of the bar, then down a narrow, dingy hallway that led past the rest rooms. Hefting his rucksack of cameras and notebooks and surveillance equipment onto his shoulder, he unlocked a heavy door at the end of the hall, pausing to turn off the security system before heading up a steep flight of stairs.

Halfway up the steps he realized he was grumbling, muttering bad-temperedly to himself. He had to cut that out. He was talking to himself too often lately. People would think he was going crazy.

Damn Eddie, he thought, as he walked into the room and tossed his rucksack on a low chair upholstered in what, once upon a time, was red velvet. Eddie was sticking his nose in it again. It was those talk shows he watched in the bar all day. Made him think he was a damned amateur psychologist.

Stripping off his shirt and tossing it on the unmade bed in the corner, Murdock paused and glanced at the mirror over a battered bureau. The photograph stuck in the frame drew his eyes as it did every time he entered the one-room apartment.

Creased and worn and folded in half, the picture was of a little girl who smiled impishly at him, one pigtail standing up higher than the other. A slender white hand with long, red-painted nails rested on the girl's shoulder, but the rest of the woman was hidden from view.

He hadn't actually torn the snapshot in half—hadn't, in all honesty, been able to bring himself to do that. But he'd folded it carefully so that he'd never have to look at the woman's face again.

With a loud, deliberate clearing of his throat, Murdock turned his back on the mirror and sat down to peel off his shoes. God, he was tired. Bone-weary. Just the way he liked it.

That was the thing Eddie and his other few friends didn't understand. He wanted to work this hard. He *needed* to work like this. They believed it was out of grief, Murdock thought grimly, but he knew better. They thought he blamed himself for not being there the night of the accident—the night his wife and daughter had careened over the edge of that ravine and only his wife had walked out of the swirling snow.

They had no idea of the truth. The awful and damning truth. Because he hadn't told anyone. Not ever.

He hadn't come home to an empty house that night. Oh, he'd been around, all right. A lot longer than anyone ever knew. And because of that, he'd never been able to grieve.

No, if he was driven, it wasn't by sorrow. It was anger that drove him, the kind of raw, helpless fury that rankled and burned in a man's gut in the quiet hours late at night, never letting him rest.

Eddie didn't know what the hell he was talking about, Murdock told himself as he stepped under the shower and closed his eyes against the jet of hot water that washed over him. He didn't need help. He didn't need or want *anyone*. Not anymore. Not ever again. He was doing just fine all on his own, and that was the way he liked it. A lone wolf, doing his job with the steady concentration of a solitary predator.

Briefly, the image of the young woman who'd gotten in his car tonight flickered in his mind. He saw again that fresh, creamy complexion and those lovely green eyes, so bright and lively. He remembered how infectious her smile had been, as vivacious and happy as a child's.

Damned woman, Murdock thought. With a snort, he turned off the shower and grabbed a towel. Her silly games could have cost him the case. Irritated all over again, he grumbled under his breath. What kind of fool let a greenhorn like her play detective, anyway?

Grudgingly, he admitted that at least she had spirit. A sort of naive gumption, he quickly amended, that would probably land her in more trouble than it saved her from. No one that trusting and inexperienced— certainly no female that gorgeous—would last long on the streets.

Raking his hands through his wet hair, Murdock scowled at the foggy mirror above the little sink. One thing was certain. He was going to keep his eye on her.

But not, he added quickly, because he wanted to protect her from getting her innocent little toes stomped on out in the big bad world. No, he'd watch her damned close because she was on his turf, meddling in his case. And he wanted to know why. That was his business. That was his job. And he *would* find out, Murdock promised himself.

WITH A WEARY GROAN, Georgie pressed her flushed cheek against the cold tile of the bathroom wall . . . and moaned some more. Her forehead was clammy, her head ached and her stomach was doing double back-ward-somersaults. What a way to start the day, she complained silently.

On her first day of work at Poulopoulos Investigations, she'd felt ill in the morning. But that was under-standable. She'd been a nervous wreck during every final exam she'd ever written. The stress of graduat-ing, breaking up with Stuart the Rat Lice, and begging Uncle Nikos to give her a chance at the agency must have simply been too much for her. She'd probably given herself an ulcer this time.

Still, Georgie grumbled as she gingerly picked her-self up off the bathroom floor, it didn't seem quite fair for her nerves to be acting up so violently after two whole weeks on the job, no matter how anxious she was about impressing Uncle Nikos.

And anxious was precisely what she was, Georgie admitted. Her continued employment at the agency was by no means a sure thing. Her family was not crazy about her new career. And after all, Nikos *was* a relative, much as some of the family hated to admit it. At any moment, he could knuckle under to familial pressure and fire her.

If he did, she could hardly blame him. That the entire Poulopoulos clan had managed to come to *any* consensus was nothing to sneeze at. United in the opinion that private investigating was definitely not a suitable job for a woman, the only thing that kept the family from swooping down on Nikos en masse was Georgie's threat to find another position in a different agency.

And they knew she meant it. The first time she heard that Uncle Nikos owned a detective agency, she'd made up her mind that she was going to be a private investigator. She'd been nine years old at the time, and unfortunately the idea hadn't grown on her parents in the years that followed. It had taken a degree in criminal psychology to convince her family that she was determined—although her threat to apply for that job as a prison psychologist at the Joliet State Penitentiary had also impressed them.

Wandering through her rambling old apartment with its creaky wooden floors covered in bright throw rugs, Georgie paused to take several deep, therapeutic breaths. There was no reason to get so overwrought, she reassured herself as she struggled into a pair of blue jeans that seemed to have shrunk a bit in the last wash.

She was doing fine at the job. Nikos was used to dealing with the family. Everything was going to be all right.

Pulling on a generously cut suit jacket and loosely knotting a man's tie through the open neck of her shirt, Georgie considered her reflection in the full-length mirror behind the bedroom door. Stylish but practical, she finally ruled, and grabbed her trench coat from the neatly made four-poster bed, a relic from her grandparents' house, like most of the furniture in her apartment.

As she headed through the old apartment, her stomach gave another rebellious heave.

"Shut up," Georgie told it. "I'm going to be late, as it is. You're just going to have to settle down."

Yet, all the way across town to her parents' house, her pulse fluttered and her insides gurgled. By the time she pulled into the driveway of the two-story brick house, she'd already chewed four antacids.

"Hello, everybody!" Georgie shouted as she walked through the back door and into the kitchen. "It's me."

In the dining room, half of her large, boisterous family was talking over breakfast. Two of her older brothers, Stefan and Demetri, were dressed for work in the gray uniforms of Poulopoulos and Sons Electrical Supplies and Service. Shoveling eggs into their mouths, they listened as her younger brother argued with her father about the previous day's Cubs game.

Her eldest brother and two older sisters were presumably at their respective homes, although Georgie would be surprised if they, too, didn't stop by sometime before lunch. For as long as she could remember, her parents' house had been crowded with people and filled with noise, practically rocking on its foundations with the laughter, shouting and bickering of a family of nine.

"Hi, Dad," Georgie said, bending over her father to kiss his rough cheek.

Dark and heavyset, muscular from years of manual work, Cosmo Poulopoulos commanded an imposing presence—behind which, she knew, lurked a marshmallow heart. He grunted at her kiss.

"Aren't you working today?" A flicker of hope lit his face. "Did you give up the job?"

Georgie sighed, then warily glanced down the table to her mother. "No, I didn't give up the job. I'm on my way there now. I just stopped by to pick up that dress Aunt Barbara wanted to borrow from Mom. I'm running a little late but—"

"What's ailing you?" Maggie Poulopoulos demanded sharply, her Irish lilt even more pronounced this morning. "You don't look long for this world."

"I'm fine, Mom," Georgie said, relieved that her mother was finally speaking to her again after a week of disapproving silence. "Really, I am. Is that a new hairstyle? It's nice."

Maggie patted at the soft, auburn curls that framed her long face. In her conservative tweed skirt and twin set she looked a bit like the Queen Mother in her early years. Georgie's own rather slipshod appearance, she knew, had always been a source of baffled disappointment to her mother.

Regrettably, Maggie was not going to be distracted by compliments this morning.

"What's the trouble with you, Georgie? Sure, you're looking as white as a boiled potato. It'll be this—" Maggie seemed to steel herself to say the word "—this terrible *detecting*, right enough. I don't know what—

ever that uncle of yours could be thinking of. 'Tis a
scandal, to be sure. The job'll be ruining your health."

"Mom," Georgie protested. "The job is fine. I like
working with—"

But her mother had already turned to glare at her father. "Sure, it's a wonder you can abide this. You should
have spoken to Nikos weeks ago. Whose brother is the
man, if he isn't yours? Just look at the child, struggling
to do a job the good Lord never intended for a woman.
She's ailing, I'm telling you. Ah, it breaks my heart,
sure."

Georgie glanced down at herself. "I don't think I look
that bad. Maybe it's the jeans. They did feel a little snug
this—"

The loud thud of her father's palm slamming down
on the table stopped her.

"And what do you want me to do, woman?" Cosmo
demanded of his wife. "If I talk to him, then what? You
want her to go work for some stranger? She's better off
with Nikos if she won't come to work in the office like
her sisters did."

"They only did that till their weddings," Georgie
said. "I'm not planning on—"

"Better off with that blackhearted heathen?" Maggie snapped, eyeing her husband haughtily. "How can
you be saying such a thing? Your family it is that's lead-
ing her astray. Private detectives! I never heard such
nonsense. Sure, if your brother was anything but a detective, none of this would have happened. You have a
responsibility, you do, Cosmo Poulopoulos. She'll be
wasting away before my eyes until you talk to your
brother, the good Lord forgive him. Look at her now.
You can see for yourself how thin she is."

"Actually—" Georgie tried to break in again "—I think I've put on a few pounds since I—"

"*My* family?" Cosmo bellowed. "Why is everything always *my* family's fault? What about your family? It was *your* sister who encouraged her to go to that college . . ."

Georgie sighed deeply. Her parents were at it again. As far as she knew, they had argued and fought throughout their entire marriage. The only thing they'd ever agreed on was that neither wanted her to be a P.I. And even then, they couldn't agree to agree. When they'd ever found time to have seven children was anyone's guess. Yet oddly enough, Georgie knew, they were passionately devoted to each other. The few times her parents had been apart, they'd both been utterly miserable.

"I don't know," her brother Stefan said, ignoring the heated battle being conducted across the table. "I think Georgie looks nice."

She gave him a grateful smile.

"She's wearing a tie," Demetri said, glancing up in disapproval from his plate.

"What's wrong with that?" Georgie retorted. "It's not one of yours."

"Georgie? Hey, Georgie," her twelve-year-old brother Anthony called, peering under the arm Cosmo had dramatically flung out to emphasize the point he was making. "Did you catch any bad guys yet?"

Georgie grinned. "Not yet. I'm still working on it."

"You want to borrow my gun?" he asked, shoveling up a spoonful of cereal. "It's a .357 Magnum. That'd scare 'em, huh?"

From the end of the table, Maggie gave an anguished shriek. "Faith and begorra! Did you hear that, Cosmo? Did you hear what your wee son was just saying?"

"Ah, Mom," Anthony grumbled. "It doesn't even have real bullets."

"First Georgie, now my baby. If you won't do something about this, Cosmo, I'll be doing it misself. I swear that brother of yours will destroy this family, sure as I'm sitting..."

"You want some breakfast, Georgie?" Stefan asked, scooting back his chair.

"And he can just be staying away from Thanksgiving dinner this fine year," Maggie continued, raising her voice over Cosmo's bellows. "I'll not be serving the likes of him, a man who corrupts the innocent souls of children who..."

Georgie glanced at the serving platter of eggs and bacon, and shuddered. "No, thanks. I don't have time. I need to get that dress and—"

"What?" Sharp-eared, Maggie paused in her tirade to turn toward her. "What was that I heard you say? Of course you'll be eating this lovely breakfast. Sit down now. How can you hope to last another day without a good breakfast in yourself?"

"Mom," Georgie protested. "I'm not hungry right—"

"That's done it." Maggie threw her napkin down. "I'm calling the doctor."

"Now, Mother—"

"Maybe you'll be listening to him if you won't pay any heed to your own poor mother." Maggie glared fiercely down the table. "And if there's anything that's seriously the matter with her, the good Lord will hold you responsible, Cosmo."

Georgie threw up her arms in exasperation as her mother headed for the phone. Stefan sent her a look of sympathy.

"I give up," Georgie cried to no one in particular. "This whole family's crazy."

"We're loony-tunes," Anthony agreed happily, raising his cereal bowl to his mouth to drink the remaining milk.

"Georgie," Cosmo said, giving her his sternest look, "I want you to give up this detective business."

Georgie nodded and patted his shoulder. "I know you do, Dad. But I can't talk about it now. I'm going to be late. Somebody, quick! Tell me where that blue dress is before Mom gets back."

IT WAS NEARLY nine-thirty when Georgie finally stopped the Volkswagen in the parking lot of the Waylon Building and raced up the stairs to fall, panting, through the glazed double doors of Poulopoulos Investigations.

Annie Dice, her uncle's longtime secretary, gave her a smile of encouragement. "Good morning," she said cheerfully. "Don't panic, but the Grand Pooh-bah himself requests your presence."

"My uncle wants to see me?"

"In his office. Pronto."

Georgie groaned. "I guess I shouldn't be surprised. It's been that kind of morning."

At the door to her uncle's office, Georgie smoothed a hand over her dark hair, which she'd plaited that morning in a thick braid that fell almost to her shoulder blades. Taking a breath, she knocked.

Nikos looked up from his paper-strewn desk when she entered and eyed her unsmilingly. He was a big man, larger than his brother Cosmo, and more prone to fits of melancholy. His black eyes were shadowed with dark circles, and his hawk nose was impressive.

"Georgie," he said simply.

"Sorry I'm late," Georgie said cheerfully. She held out the dress. "Aunt Barbara wanted to wear Mom's blue dress to the concert tonight."

Laying the dress carefully across a chair, she continued in the same light voice. "I've got some news on the Jimmy Ray Thompson case. Some very *interesting* news."

"So have I," Nikos said. He leaned back in his chair. "That's what I wanted to see you about. You're off the case."

For a long, dismayed moment Georgie stared open-mouthed at her uncle. Then she hardened her jaw.

"For heaven's sake, it was only one morning," she said. "I won't be late again. And anyway, it wasn't my fault. If Aunt Barbara hadn't asked me to—"

Nikos shook his head, and Georgie thought she detected the tiniest of smiles on his lips. "It has nothing to do with that."

"It doesn't?"

"Although I hope you keep your word. This business demands punctuality."

Baffled, Georgie blinked at him. "Then why are you taking me off the case?"

"Because, my dear niece, there is no case. Not anymore."

Bewildered, Georgie glanced around the cluttered office as though it might hold a clue for her. "Okay, I give up. Why isn't there a case any longer?"

"Because we don't have a client." Nikos picked up the morning newspaper and tossed it across the desk toward her. "Howard Kavin was fished out of the Chicago River late last night. Very wet. Very drunk. And very, very dead."

IN THE SMALL seedy tavern, Georgie sat at a corner booth under a shaded light, nursing a lukewarm cup of coffee and mumbling angrily under her breath. When her uncle's news had finally filtered through to her, she'd tried to argue with him. If Howard Kavin was dead, she'd asked, didn't it seem the tiniest bit suspicious? And what about this Murdock character, who was also watching Jimmy Ray? Shouldn't they at least try to find out why? Shouldn't they try to find out what had happened?

Nikos had only smiled tolerantly. No client meant no fee, he'd replied. And no fee meant no case. They weren't in the business for their health, he'd reminded her. She'd tried to combat his decision with reminders about justice, civic duty and plain old-fashioned curiosity, but he'd shrugged off every argument.

That was her uncle for you, Georgie thought in annoyance. Despite her awe of his profession, Uncle Nikos had never been her favorite relative. If her own father was generous to a fault, Nikos had retaliated by displaying an equally exaggerated propensity for avarice. A simple case of sibling rivalry, Georgie decided.

Now she sat in the drab little tavern, watching as it slowly filled with locals, mostly hardworking laborers from the nearby docks and the canning factory down the street. If she could prove that Howard Kavin's death was as suspicious as it sounded, it could be her first big case. She'd solve the mystery, and Uncle Nikos would be so impressed, he'd make her the star investigator of Poulopoulos, Inc. She'd be assigned to all the most glamorous, most exciting cases. Maybe she'd even get a raise and her own desk.

Lost in daydreams of the Mata Hari-like life-style she'd soon be living, Georgie buried her nose in her coffee mug and absently took a swallow of the acrid brew. With a grimace, she lowered the cup just as a shadow fell ominously over her table.

"What the hell," said a low male voice.

Squinting against the light from the overhanging lamp, Georgie smiled tentatively. "Hi, there."

Murdock stared at her with amazement and horror. Once again he wore the concealing hat low over his forehead, and his long overcoat looked as if he'd slept in it. He probably had, Georgie decided. Under the coat, his white shirt and khaki dress pants were wrinkled, and a loosened tie hung halfway down his chest. Yes, Georgie confirmed, he was a man who would definitely sleep with his boots on...scuffed cowboy boots, to be precise.

"What are you doing here?" he demanded at last. "How did you find out about this place?"

Swallowing hard, Georgie answered carefully, realizing how very important it was that she not blow this interview. He was her only chance, she told herself. If Murdock didn't trust her, she really *wouldn't* have a case.

"I got your address from the licensing bureau."

"That's privileged information. It's private."

Her small smile was apologetic. "Yes, well. A friend of my uncle works there. A distant cousin, actually."

He was silent for a long minute. "You seem to have a lot of relatives."

"Oh, yes," Georgie agreed, a little more hopefully. "That's one thing I'm not short of."

Glancing around as though checking that no one was watching, he seemed to come to a decision. With a suspicious glower he sat down opposite her, placing a heavy backpack on the floor beside him and folding his large hands on the table. Georgie noticed he was careful to lean back and out of the dim circle of light created by the lamp above the table.

"What do you want?"

Taken aback by the abruptness of his tone, Georgie blinked at him. "Want?"

"Yes, want. This isn't a social call, I take it. You want something."

"Oh. Well." Nervously, Georgie fingered the knot of her tie. "All right. Yes, I do want something. You're right."

In the shadows, his handsome face was cool and impassive.

"The truth is—" Georgie nervously cleared her throat. "I want to work with you."

3

FOR WHAT SEEMED to Georgie like a decade, Murdock stared at her in absolute silence with an expressionless face. A moth flew against the bulb of the light overhead, its tiny wings beating the stale, smoky air. Rough male laughter erupted from the crowd by the bar. Georgie gripped her coffee mug tighter.

Finally, Murdock's lips moved. Slowly, very slowly, they turned upward in that wide, roguish smile that carried something wicked in its steadiness. Without a word, he grabbed the rucksack and pushed back his chair.

Georgie's face fell in dismay. "Wait," she cried. Reaching out, she closed her fingers over the hand he rested on the table.

Under her palm his powerful fist lay still and unmoving. His skin was warm, and she felt the tension in him so vividly it seemed to seep from his fingers and into hers, tingling up her arm.

Motionless and unsmiling, he sat on the edge of his seat, staring down at the hand she'd laid across his. His stare was so intense that, after a stunned moment, Georgie snatched her hand away.

When she did, he looked across at her with shadowed eyes.

"Just listen to me for a second," Georgie urged.

He made an impatient move as though to rise.

"Please. Just give me a chance," she pleaded. "It's important."

He shook his head as if dismissing her and her incredible foolishness. Then he rose.

"For heaven's sake," Georgie burst out angrily. "You are the rudest, most aggravating, absolutely impossible man. The least you could do is hear me out."

He paused by the table, his backpack clutched in his hand. "I'm not interested," he said curtly.

"Oh, really?" Georgie scrambled to the end of the booth. "You don't care that Howard Kavin's dead?"

For a second, Georgie thought he might continue to walk away. When he suddenly halted and turned to scowl at her, her heart gave a tiny leap of triumph. She'd gambled and won. What real detective could have walked away from a statement like that?

"I thought that might get your attention," she said with satisfaction.

She watched him hesitate. The lines in his craggy face were more defined tonight, and for the first time she realized his gray eyes were dark with weariness. He looked, she imagined fancifully, like a man plagued by nightmares. Despite his rigid, wooden glower, her heart softened at the exhaustion etched in his face.

"Won't you please listen now to what I have to say?" she asked more gently.

He inclined his head, but he didn't sit down again. "I'm listening. But it better be good. I don't know any Howard Kavin."

"You don't?" Surprise colored Georgie's voice. "But I thought you— Never mind. That doesn't matter. He was my client. He was the reason I was watching Jimmy Ray. And now he's dead. The official report is that he was drunk and fell in the Chicago River, but—"

"But you don't buy that."

"No." Georgie gave him a close look. "Would you?"

Gray eyes, sharp and intense behind a cloud of exhaustion, studied her dispassionately. Suddenly, he strode back to the booth and sat down.

"No," he finally replied. "Probably not." A frown creased his forehead as he considered the problem.

She'd hooked him, Georgie thought jubilantly. He was interested. In the flood of relief that overcame her, she almost missed his next words.

"But what does this have to do with my case? Why come to me?"

Less sure of herself on this point, Georgie spoke hesitantly. "Because you're watching Jimmy Ray, too. Which is odd enough in itself, don't you think?" She took a deep breath, then spilled the beans. "Howard Kavin wanted us to tail the guy and collect any dirt we could on him. Kavin's daughter has been dating Jimmy Ray, and he wanted to put a stop to the relationship. We were supposed to gather the ammo. Now that Howard Kavin's dead, I've been pulled off the case. I just want a chance to find out what happened to him."

Murdock's frown deepened, but she could tell he was listening closely.

"Does your client, by any chance," she ventured, "have a daughter, too?"

Turning his head, he gazed across the room, and Georgie saw the taut muscles in his neck move as he swallowed. But when he looked back, his forehead was smooth and unfurrowed.

"No," he said brusquely.

She waited, but he obviously didn't intend to divulge any more information, not about *his* case, at any rate.

"You're barking up the wrong tree," he said at last. "And if you think Jimmy Ray might have knocked off your client, you can forget it. He didn't leave his place all night. I can vouch for that."

"But Kavin's death might have something to do with your client?"

As though a shutter had fallen across his eyes, Murdock gazed at her in obstinate silence.

"Right," Georgie said, disappointed. "You're not talking."

He picked up his backpack for the second time. "Mind if I go now?"

Wincing inwardly at the sarcasm in his voice, Georgie persisted. "What about my working with you? You don't have to tell me anything about your case if you don't want to. That's fine with me. But give me a chance to find out what happened to Howard Kavin. I could help you watch Jimmy Ray at night after I get off work. I could take the weekends for you."

A ghost of his disturbingly rakish smile touched his lips. "Not a chance in hell, lady."

"But why?" Georgie pressed. "I bet you could use the help."

"I work alone." Swinging the backpack onto his broad shoulder, he added, "Take my advice and forget about Howard Kavin. Forget about Jimmy Ray. And if you really want to be smart, get out of this business altogether—"

"Out of the—"

"Before you blunder your pretty little way into a mess you can't handle and get yourself hurt."

Georgie felt her cheeks flush with angry heat and she opened her mouth to retort, but he was already swinging away from the booth, walking with a slightly rolling stride down a narrow hallway. Choking and stammering with indignation, it took her a moment to recover her voice.

"Oh, yeah?" she sputtered after him. "Well . . . well, we'll just see about that! Mr. *Know*-It-All."

But he was already down the hall and out of earshot.

ACROSS THE STREET from Eddie's Tavern, Georgie slumped behind the wheel of her Volkswagen, a floppy white canvas hat pulled low over her forehead and *Psychologic Profile of a Serial Killer* open in front of her face. When Murdock finally pushed through the door of Eddie's Tavern, she watched over the top of her book as he paused on the stoop.

He'd changed his wrinkled white button-down shirt and shabby old overcoat for a black turtleneck and leather jacket that made him look dark, mysterious and dangerously handsome. Thank goodness, she wasn't susceptible to *that* kind of attraction. Stuart the Rat Lice had effectively cured her of any such nonsense. Romantic attachments, she had decided, were far too humiliating and painful for her to repeat *that* mistake any time soon.

Yet, peering over her textbook at Murdock, Georgie noticed how gallant he looked standing there alone on the sidewalk, as heroic and fierce as a Viking, with his chiseled profile turned toward her and his thick, sandy-blond hair blown by the wind as though he . . . She forced a short, disdainful snort and rolled her eyes in a show of scorn. What a load of drivel, she told herself firmly. Viking, indeed!

When Murdock glanced cautiously across the street in her direction, Georgie slid down farther in her seat, furtively pulling her hat an inch lower. Narrow-eyed, she watched him stroll across the street to his car. He sure was taking his own sweet time about it, she thought in annoyance.

Finally, the Buick pulled away from the curb, and Georgie sat up. Starting her car, she followed stealthily behind, a smile playing on her lips.

"We'll see who's the blundering amateur now, won't we?" she said aloud with a short laugh. "I'm onto you, Mr. High-and-Mighty. You won't get away from *me* so easily."

IN THE ELEVATOR of a downtown parking garage, Murdock smiled quietly to himself, humming a low, tuneless song. Stopping his car at the ground level, he got out, paused as if to get his bearings, then headed toward the crowded sidewalk.

At a busy open-air mall he hesitated again, then with sudden decision, started down the broad walkway between the shops and restaurants, stopping now and then to peer into a storefront window. At the far end of the mall, he came out onto an immense plaza. There he suddenly broke into a quick, purposeful jog.

Dashing between clusters of after-work shoppers, skirting a fountain of fat, marble cherubs and weaving his way through rows of wooden benches dotted with pigeons, he finally reached the other side of the plaza and skidded around the corner of a government building.

Deep in the shadows of the building's vast portico, he leaned against a pillar, catching his breath and listening to the echoes of footsteps and voices around him. In the plaza below, a pigeon cooed, and he heard a flurry of wings as the flock rose into the air.

He didn't have long to wait. Within moments, quick, light footfalls sounded on the marble tile, ringing hollowly high above in the great vaulted ceiling. Murdock stiffened in readiness, his muscles taut and tensed.

The instant she drew near enough, he leaped out and pinned her wrists behind her back with one hand, pressing her cheek against the marble pillar before she could utter a single gasp.

"What are you doing?" he demanded in a low, threatening voice. "Did you really think you could follow me without my knowing it?"

A faint, breathy moan was her only answer, and he loosened his grip on her wrists. Still wordless, she sagged against him, her slight body trembling under his hands.

Surprise made him go still. Against the warm dark brown of her hair, her face looked pinched and white as a sheet. Weakly she leaned against him and gave a small, soft groan.

Uneasiness stirred in him. He'd wanted to scare her. He'd meant to teach her a lesson and knock some sense into her foolhardy little head. But he hadn't meant to frighten her this badly.

"Hey," he called, gripping her slender shoulders and bending down to peer at her face. "Are you all right? Get a grip on yourself."

"Uh-oh," she whispered. "I think I'm going to be sick."

"Sick?"

"Yes, sick," she snapped, some of the fight back in her voice. "I'm going to throw up."

"Good Lord," Murdock muttered just as she swayed under his hands.

When her knees buckled and she started to sink to the marble tile, he had to haul her up by her armpits. Half carrying, half propelling her, he led her to the edge of the portico. There he plunked her down on the nearest step, clenching his jaw and fighting unsuccessfully against an unexpected rush of guilt.

How could he have known she'd react this way? he wanted to protest.

More gently, he rested a hand on the back of her neck and squatted beside her.

"Put your head between your knees," he said. "You'll feel better in a moment."

"I won't feel better," she retorted testily, but she obeyed him, anyway.

"My nerves are shot," she went on irritably, peering up at him. "You scared me to death."

"I'm sorry," Murdock said, and realized with surprise that he meant it. He pushed her head back down.

"Sorry? A fat lot of good that does me," she muttered ungraciously, her voice muffled. Fumbling in the pocket of her trench coat, she pulled out a half-eaten roll of antacids and popped one in her mouth.

Wary and alert, he watched her chew, trying to ignore the satiny feel of her hair under his fingers and the appealing scent of fresh powder and soap from her skin.

"Let me up," she said after crunching a second tablet. She wiggled under his hand. "I'm okay now. It passed."

"Are you sure?"

"Yes, I'm sure. Let go of me."

She sat up, and he watched her brush several stray strands of silky brown hair from her cheeks and readjust her shirt with a sharp tug. Sinking to the step, he sat beside her and gazed out at the pigeons strutting in the plaza. Silently he waited.

She was being awfully quiet, he thought. Sneaking a peek at her, he saw she was watching him, her large, luminous green eyes regaining some of their normal sparkle.

"How long did you know?" she finally asked.

"That you were following me? Since we left Eddie's."

She moaned aloud, and he glanced apprehensively at her, half expecting her to turn a greenish white again.

"I wanted to see what you were up to." Her tone was reluctant.

"Obviously," he said dryly.

"I think there's something fishy going on."

"Fishy?"

"Howard Kavin didn't just fall into the river. I'd bet anything on it. Don't ask me why, but I'm sure of it."

"Women's intuition?"

Missing—or choosing to ignore—his sarcasm, she nodded. "If you want to call it that. Oh, don't you see? If I'm going to get to the bottom of this, I need your help."

He looked down at his hands. Why did she have to be so blatantly, so artlessly sincere? he asked himself with a scowl. Why did she have to look at him with such trusting eyes? Deception and lies he could handle. They were part of his world, and he lived effortlessly with them every day of his life. But *this*, this clear-eyed decency of hers was more than he was equipped for. He was out of his depth.

"Why?" he asked, letting the suspicion in his voice show. "Why do you care? What's this Kavin guy to you?"

"Well," she began thoughtfully. Her green eyes were on his, honest and frank. With a tiny frown, she considered his question, then answered slowly. "Call it an overactive sense of moral duty. I don't know. That day in the office, Howard Kavin was, well, timid. Almost frightened. You could tell right away that he was one of the weak ones. A nobody. The kind of man other people forget."

Her eyes clouded. "That's why I can't let it drop. Somebody has to care that he died. Somebody has to remember him and try to do something about it. Do you understand?"

Murdock felt a sinking sensation in the pit of his stomach. "Yes, I understand. I don't agree. But I guess I understand how you feel."

A little more reluctantly she added, "Also, this case is important to me for another reason. I *need* to do a good job." She paused for a moment before going on, "Oh, can't you see? There's just too many strange things about it. I know there's something more going on. Jimmy Ray, for starters. What are the chances of two separate investigators watching the same man?"

"Plenty," he said shortly. After a pause, he continued unhappily, "Look, most of the suspects I watch aren't your average, law-abiding citizens. And if a man's up to one game, you can bet he's had a hand in one or two others. Now or in the past."

"Game? What kind of game?" she asked, jumping instantly on his choice of words.

With a sigh, Murdock rubbed a hand over his face. "You don't give up easily, do you?"

"Nope."

The smile she beamed at him was so sweet and completely candid that his heart gave a ruthless, almost painful twist. For one insane moment, he nearly raised his hand and touched her face. Turning away abruptly, he studied the plaza.

"You *do* sort of owe me one," she said playfully. "I mean, after scaring the living daylights out of me."

He could get up and walk away from her, he thought. Just stand up and walk down the stairs. That was what he should do. That was what he *wanted* to do, he corrected himself quickly.

But he knew in his heart it was too late. He'd become fascinated, drawn like a parched man to water. It was his own fault. It had been so damned long since he'd let anything light or good into his life that he'd almost forgotten what it looked like. Like a backwoods yokel at a carnival, gaping in openmouthed astonishment at the strange and exotic wonders on display, he couldn't have looked away from her if he'd tried.

The knowledge needled him, and he nearly sprang to his feet.

"Murdock?"

And yet, he countered, if he left her now, who knew what kind of trouble she might get into on her own? He had the sneaking suspicion that he was fishing for excuses, but he couldn't deny the truth of that concern. She was bound to run headlong into something nasty — because, for all her naiveté, she'd nearly convinced him that something odd *was* going on.

"Murdock?" she repeated, bending her head to peep into his face.

He cleared his throat, avoiding her eyes. "All right. I'll see what I can find out," he said gruffly.

She nearly leaped from the step with joy. "Really? You mean it?"

"But just this one time. And I work alone," he admonished, trying to ignore the charm of her elation. "Alone. Got it?"

"Of course. Of course. Whatever you say."

His eyes narrowed distrustfully at her ready compliance. "All right. As long as that's understood. I'll tell you right now, though, there's probably nothing in it. If there is, I'll find it. And if *I* think it's relevant, I'll let you know."

"Okay."

"In return, you keep your nose out of it," he said sternly, and saw her smile fade. "I mean it. No more meddling. And no more following me around."

"I'm a private investigator. I'm supposed to meddle."

"Not in my business, you aren't," he retorted and rose to his feet.

"Where are you going?"

"To keep the meeting you almost made me late for."

"Meeting? With who?"

Hands on his hips, he looked down at her. "That's none of your business. You promised, remember?"

"All right." She sighed but not too unhappily. "I promised."

"Make sure you keep it," he said and started to turn away. She was watching him with wide, trusting eyes, and before he knew what he was doing, he paused and added more kindly, "You know, with a little experience, you probably wouldn't make a half-bad detective."

The gratified smile that threatened to break out on her lips made him instantly regret his words.

"But until then," he warned, "you could get yourself into some serious trouble. Don't play with fire until you learn how to handle it."

Without waiting for her reply, he headed down the stairs. With every step, he could feel her eyes on him, burning the back of his scalp. And with every step, he tried to push down the warm, unfamiliar happiness that threatened to bubble up in him.

Damn her, he thought, though he felt his lips twitch in a smile. She was one helluva nuisance, a real thorn in his side, he told himself.

Yet by the time he'd retraced his steps to the parking garage and his car, he was humming the tuneless melody again.

THEY WERE STANDING together in the plaza in the rain, locked in an embrace so tight that she could feel his heart beating under her cheek.

"Murdock," Georgie murmured, and raised her face for his kiss. Firm, tender lips met hers, and she sighed with delight. Somewhere in the building behind them, a clock struck the time and suddenly she felt the scratchy, disagreeable roughness of a beard.

Startled, she pulled back and gasped. Behind the distinguished, faintly graying beard, Stuart Whitmore smiled coldly down at her. He was dressed in one of the genteel tweed jackets she'd seen him wear so often for his wildly popular lectures. When he smiled, he exhaled blue clouds of pipe smoke.

"It was just one night, my dear," he said with a cruel laugh. "You didn't really expect anything more, did you?"

"Oh!" Georgie cried in disgust, and tried to free herself from his arms. The clock on the government

building struck again and again, ringing maddeningly in her ears as she struggled against Stuart's octopus-like arms.

"Here, take a copy of my latest book. I've auto-graphed it just for you."

"Help!" she cried aloud and, clawing at the twisted sheets on her bed, she woke up with a start.

On the night table beside her, the phone rang again and Georgie stared at it, breathing hard.

"Good heavens," she breathed and ran a shaky hand through her hair as she reached for the receiver. "What? Yes? Who is it?"

A long silence answered her, then finally she heard, "Georgie? Umm, Georgie Pil . . . er, Polli—"

Georgie's cheeks flamed as his voice invoked a memory of her dream. Desperately, she attempted to gather her thoughts. "Poulopoulos. Yes, it's me. Murdock?"

"Yeah, it's—"

"What time is it?"

"Time? Uh, nine-thirty."

"Nine what!" Sitting up, Georgie grabbed for her alarm clock, knocking it over instead. "It is? I must have overslept. I . . ."

A sudden wave of nausea swept over her. "Can you call back?"

"What?"

"I have to go. Call me back."

"I'm at a pay phone. Listen, I might have found something."

"Murdock—"

"I've got a meeting with a guy I know on the force at eleven if you want to tag along. We'll call it even then."

"Really," she cried. "I have to go now."

"I'll be by in about an hour. I think you'll—"

Slamming down the phone and holding her hand to her mouth, Georgie dashed for the bathroom, cursing all the way.

WHEN GEORGIE ANSWERED the door of her apartment at ten-thirty, Murdock stood in the hall, filling the space with his broad, muscular shoulders. He wore the shabby overcoat and battered felt hat and was frowning, as usual. His scowl deepened when he saw her.

"How did you get my number?" Georgie demanded, in no mood for pleasantries this morning. "Don't tell me you have a relative at the licensing bureau, too."

"No." At her tone, his face had grown wary. "I looked it up. You're in the phone book."

"Oh." Deflated, Georgie grimaced, then threw the door open. "Well, since you're here, you'd better come in."

He took off his hat, and laid it carefully on a chair by the door, hesitating a moment before following her into the living room.

"Georgie—"

"Don't ask," she snapped. "I don't know what's wrong."

"You don't look so good."

"Thanks a million." She took in his crumpled tie, disheveled hair and unshaved jaw. "*You*, on the other hand, are a vision of loveliness."

If she hadn't felt so miserable, she might have thought the confused look that came over his face was funny. Who would have thought that Murdock the Tough Guy could look so uncertain?

Instead, she dropped to the edge of the couch and immediately burst into tears.

"I think I'm having a nervous breakdown," she said, sobbing.

Large and awkward, Murdock stood beside the couch with a horrified look on his face. "What're you doing? Don't do that," he complained in a gruff voice. "Don't cry like that."

"I can't help it," she wailed. "I feel like a wreck. I *look* like a wreck. I'm losing my mind. And on top of that, I'm ugly and fat and . . . and horrid-looking."

"No, you aren't," he said clumsily. "I mean, you look all right to me."

"All right?" She turned a tear-streaked face up to him. "That's supposed to make me feel better? Just *all right*? Who wants to look just *all right*?"

Hastily, he blundered bravely forward. "Not *just* all right. You look . . . you look great. Really nice. Sort of, well, sexy."

Holding a tissue to her nose, Georgie blinked. "Ah do?"

"Yeah. Sure, you do."

"You're jus' saying thad," she accused stuffily, and blew her nose. "Jus' to be nice."

"No, I'm not. I thought you were sexy the moment I saw you." As soon as the words were out of his mouth, a strange look of astonished horror came over Murdock's face, as though he'd just that moment realized something terrible.

Georgie stared at him. "You did?"

His forehead was knit in an agony of bewilderment. "Well, yeah. I mean, I don't know. I guess so. Sort of."

"Oh, wonderful," she blubbered in a tear-choked voice. She pulled another tissue from the box on the coffee table.

"Well, for God's sake," he suddenly burst out. "A man would have to be blind not to think so."

"You would?" She sniffled. "I mean, he would?"

Uneasily, Murdock stepped back from the couch, turning away and folding his brawny arms. From where she sat, Georgie could see a muscle jump in his jaw. He looked baffled and angry and completely at sea.

Raking a hand through his mussy hair, he suddenly turned back and raised a finger to point at her. "Look here," he began brusquely.

She waited, and saw him waver uncertainly. He dropped his hand. Less forcefully, he went on, "You . . . you've got to stop this, er, this crying."

Georgie nodded and tried to suppress a small hiccuped sob. "I know."

"Well, stop then."

"I *can't*. You can't ask me to just stop like that."

Wheeling in frustration, he looked up at the ceiling, and she heard him mutter, "Women. My God. Women. I'll never get it."

"I'm sorry," Georgie cried into her tissue. "I don't know what's wrong with me. I'm just so miserable. It's so stupid. Fighting with my family over being a detective... And then having to practically beg Uncle Nikos for . . . And there was this horrible, really awful relationship. Not really a relationship. Just this stupid infatuation that barely lasted a day. But he was so famous, and everyone admired him so much, and how did I know he was such a complete and total jerk? Oh, God! Why am I telling you all this?"

He was watching her with a look of extreme discomfort—shocked, she guessed, at her outburst.

"It sounds so ridiculous when I say it out loud." She tried to smile and failed. "I'm not usually such a cry-baby. Really, I'm not. But the truth is . . . the truth is, sometimes lately I just feel so . . . so miserable."

A fresh wave of tears threatened to overcome her, and Georgie buried her face in her tissue. She was just fumbling for another when suddenly, without warning, she was jerked to her feet. Stunned, she gasped and nearly cried out in alarm. But before she could make a sound, Murdock pulled her against him and covered her mouth with his.

Paralyzed by surprise, she felt his powerful arms encircle her, engulfing her and crushing her against the steely length of his body. His kiss was nothing like the light, gentle brushing of lips she'd imagined in her dream. Rough and hungry, forceful and deliberate, he devoured her mouth with his, stealing her breath away.

Weakly she clutched at his wrinkled shirt. Under her hands, the curves of his chest were solid and hard as stone, and his breath was hot and sweet like sugared coffee. With steady insistence he parted her lips with his tongue, and his hand on the small of her back pressed her closer in dizzyingly intimate contact with him. A gasp caught in her throat, and every nerve, every fiber of her body sprang instantly alive.

With an abandon she hadn't known she was capable of, Georgie leaned into his embrace. A tiny moan escaped her, and at the sound his kiss grew stronger, a little wilder and more fierce.

Then abruptly, he released her. Stepping back, he tilted his head and watched her sway unsteadily.

"How do you feel?" he asked, his voice husky and thick.

Georgie gaped.

"How are you now?" he insisted.

She gazed at him in astonishment. "Fine. Much better."

"Good." He raised a hand to his face and rubbed his jaw. His hand, she saw, shook slightly. "Good. Go wash your face."

"What?"

"Go on."

Still in a stupor, she blinked at him.

"Go wash your face," he repeated. "You want to miss our appointment?"

"Our what?"

"Our meeting with my friend, Orin Dobbs. Now you're feeling better, you might as well come with me."

Confused and dazed, Georgie raised a trembling finger to her mouth, unsure if she'd imagined the whole kiss or not. Her lips were reassuringly hot and tender.

Murdock's eyes followed her hand, and she saw him swallow, quick and hard. He turned away.

"So, are you coming with me? Or are you just going to stand around all day?"

Georgie gave him an odd, wondering look. "I'm coming," she said. "Believe me, I wouldn't miss it for the world."

4

SERGEANT ORIN DOBBS of the Chicago Police Department was a bullet-shaped man. Powerful, sloping shoulders that began just beneath his ears—thus circumventing the usual need for a neck—blended without any clear division into a thick trim torso and stubby legs. The torpedo image was further enhanced by his shining, hairless pate.

"Murdock," Orin said without smiling, rising to his feet as they approached his table in the busy diner. His eyes flickered questioningly over Georgie.

"Dobbs," Murdock grunted back with a sharp nod of his head.

Really, Georgie thought, men had the strangest greeting rituals. Like leery bull moose, they always seemed to eye each other first, prepared to swagger a bit and even to square off if necessary. Heaven forbid that they should act glad to see one another. Two women, on the other hand, would have already been in each other's arms and flipping through snapshots by now.

With a scowl and a jerk of his thumb, Murdock indicated Georgie, acknowledging her presence for the first time since they'd left her apartment. When she'd come out of the bathroom, he'd already gone down to the Buick where she found him sitting in stony, thoughtful silence. They'd driven to the diner without exchanging a single word. Neither had mentioned the kiss.

"Georgie Pulpit," he said now, introducing her.

Georgie darted a sour look at him.

"Poulopoulos," she corrected and stuck out her hand. "How d'you do?"

Orin shook her hand. "So you finally decided to hire another investigator, eh, Murdock? 'Bout time."

Murdock frowned. "What? No, she's just an—"

"Assistant," Georgie broke in, smiling politely.

"—acquaintance," Murdock finished, glowering at her. "But she's all right. We can talk in front of her."

Orin was looking at them strangely. "You two don't work together?"

"Oh, yes," Georgie began.

"No, we don't," Murdock snapped, shooting her a dark warning look. "She's helping me out on a case. That's all."

"It's *my* case," Georgie said between her teeth, still smiling at Orin. "Not yours."

The man, Georgie thought, was impossible. What was the matter with him? One minute he was kissing her—kissing her the way she'd never known a man could kiss a woman—and the next he could barely bring himself to acknowledge her existence. With a small mental jolt, Georgie realized those two things just might be related.

"Would you please," Murdock hissed at her from the corner of his mouth, "shut up and let me handle this?"

Orin was frowning at them in bewilderment, and Georgie gave him a sympathetic look. "It's sort of a complicated situation," she explained.

"Yeah, I guess so," the bald man said. "You've sure as hell got me confused."

"Welcome to the party," Murdock grumbled. With a final glare at Georgie, he nodded at the file on the table in front of Orin. "What did you manage to get for me?"

Pulling out a chair, Murdock sat at the table, not bothering to remove his hat, and ignoring Georgie who was left standing alone in the aisle. He was sorry he had kissed her, Georgie told herself. But that didn't mean he had to be so rude. Clenching her teeth, she wrenched out a chair and sat purposely close to him, her shoulder nearly brushing his.

"I didn't come up with much," Orin said, glancing uneasily at Georgie as she joined them. She smiled at him, and he gave a slight shrug. "Technically, we're not supposed to take files out of the station, but there's nothing in this one you couldn't read in the papers. Not that anyone's going to be interested enough in your guy to waste print space on him. Kavin wasn't exactly front-page material."

Flipping open the file, Murdock glanced quickly at the police report. Georgie scooted her chair a fraction closer and tried to peer over his arm, but he shut the file before she could read a word.

"Why don't you just run it by me then?" Murdock suggested. "His death was accidental?"

Orin looked surprised. "Yeah, sure. The guy was as plastered as a wall. Probably didn't even realize when he tumbled over the railing of the bridge."

"There was no sign of a struggle then? No marks on the body?"

Orin shrugged. "Sure, plenty. But no more than you'd expect on any corpse that'd been knocking around in a river for four hours after falling from a bridge of that height."

Georgie's stomach gave a squeamish shudder at the thought of what Kavin must have looked like when they pulled him out. Nobody deserved to die like that . . . certainly not meek, nervous little Howard Kavin.

"Suicide?" Murdock suggested.

"Eh? Sure, maybe." Orin's tone made it clear he wouldn't bet on it. "But suicides almost always follow a pattern—tidying up their lives, leaving notes, stuff like that. It's possible it was a spur-of-the-moment jump, but I doubt it."

"What about his family?" Georgie piped up. Ignoring Murdock's quick, irritated movement, she continued, "Did they know why he was out at that hour? Did they know if he'd been drinking with anyone specific?"

"Family?" Orin squinted at her, then reached for the file and thumbed through it. He shook his head. "Kavin didn't have a family. Lived alone, as far as we know. Had a room in one of those run-down hotels near the river that rent by the week, mostly to transients who can't afford much more and wouldn't want to stick around much longer if they could. Kavin, though, he'd been there almost seven years. There's always a few in those places."

Georgie gaped at the man. "That can't be right. He had a family. I *know* he had a daughter. And he lived in the suburbs out near—"

The unexpected pressure of Murdock's hand on her leg, gently but firmly squeezing her knee under the table, silenced her.

Orin shrugged. "Not the guy we fished out of the river. We had to get the super of the dump he was living in to identify him. There wasn't anyone else. No family, no employer, nothing. From the autopsy report, the sorry state of his liver pretty much explains his life history. The guy was a serious boozer. Probably would have been dead within a year, anyway."

Stunned, Georgie stared at Murdock. He refused to meet her gaze.

"Right," Murdock said briskly. "Sounds about as cut-and-dried as they come."

"It is." Orin narrowed his eyes. "Or at any rate, it was. Until you started asking me questions. What's your interest in this, Murdock? Is there something about this old bum I should know?"

"If there is, you'll have to get it from someone else. He's not our guy."

"Oh, yeah?" Orin looked skeptical. "Now, why don't I believe that?"

"Habit," Murdock answered simply. "You're a cop. Everyone lies to you."

To Georgie's surprise, Orin Dobbs merely nodded gravely in agreement. "Yeah, it's one of the hazards of our professions, isn't it? You never know who to believe. Got to be suspicious of everyone."

"I don't know what's wrong with that," Murdock replied easily. "It's kept us alive this long."

Orin smiled and shook his head. "Man, you haven't changed a bit. Not one iota. It's good to see you."

Tersely—more tersely than was polite, Georgie thought—Murdock grunted, "Yeah, well," then changed the subject. "Listen, does the name Jimmy Ray Thompson ring any bells?"

"Jimmy Ray?" Orin screwed up his face, thinking. "I don't know. Seems like I've heard that name before, but I couldn't tell you where or when. Why? You think he's connected with the Kavin death?"

"Naw. Just something else I'm working on. Thought you might be able to help."

"Sorry. If I remember anything, I'll give you a call." He watched Murdock push back his chair. "In the meantime, don't be such a stranger, huh? You know we'd love to have you over. Peggy hasn't seen your ugly mug for years."

Rising to her feet beside Murdock, Georgie could feel his discomfort in the sudden tensing of his body.

"Yeah, sure," he said noncommittally, avoiding her gaze. "Thanks for the information."

Taking Georgie's arm, he seemed determined suddenly to hustle her away.

"Seriously," Orin was saying. "If you decide to tell me the truth—or if you need any help with whatever's going on—well, you know where to find me."

Murdock nodded briskly. "Right. Sure, I will. Thanks for the help, Dobbs."

They were moving through the diner at a respectable clip, Murdock propelling her from behind. Yet Georgie still caught Orin's voice from behind them.

"You're welcome. Anytime, Lieutenant," the man called. "Anytime."

"LIEUTENANT?" she repeated. "Why 'lieutenant'?"

Hunched over the steering wheel so that his forehead nearly touched the windshield, Murdock concentrated on the road and tried his best to ignore the woman beside him. With a burst of speed, he swerved the old Buick around a laundry van and dodged between a pickup truck and a very new, very shiny BMW. The driver gave them a white-faced stare as they shot past.

He must have had a temporary lapse of sanity earlier, Murdock decided. A short, violent brainstorm or something. When he'd hauled her to her feet and kissed her this morning, it was the only thing he could think of to shut her up. What did he know about women? It seemed like the best way, and it had worked.

Yes, he'd only done it to stop her blubbering. Hadn't he? And yet all through the interview with Dobbs, he could barely think of anything else but what that kiss had been like. He was an idiot. He must have been out of his mind.

"Why 'lieutenant'?" she asked again.

"For God's sake, drop it," he grumbled, and sped through a yellow light. It was time, he knew, to ditch her. Before he made any more stupid moves. Take her to this appointment of hers, drop her off and make damned sure they never met again.

The only problem was that the taste of her still lingered, teasing him, tormenting him . . . tempting him. Well, it served him right, Murdock thought, scowling. That's what happened when a man lost control, even for a minute. He knew better than to let down his guard. Relax your vigilance for the briefest instant, and before you knew what hit you, the enemy was on you, storming your lines of defense.

It wasn't a mistake most men made twice. Certainly, he intended to make sure he didn't falter again.

"Were you a police officer, too?" she asked. "Is that why he called you lieutenant? Because you used to be in the force?"

"Oh, for the love of—" Clutching a fistful of tawny hair, he glowered at the street rushing toward them. Didn't she ever give up? "No. All right? No, I wasn't. Now give it a rest."

"So that means you must have been in the military," she mused thoughtfully.

"I said, leave it alone."

"Yes. That must be it." She nodded as though to herself. "You were in the military, weren't you?"

"It's none of your business," he said shortly. "And if you can't shut up, you can always walk to your appointment, whatever it is. Did I ask you where you're going? No, I didn't. You don't see me sticking my nose in your business."

"It's a doctor's appointment."

At his sharp look, she added, "Just a checkup. To pacify my mother. And I don't see what's so bad about admitting you were in the military. Lots of people are. In fact, most people consider it an honorable thing. Unless," she said, pausing to consider, "you were involved in something secret. Something you're not supposed to talk about."

He could see her mind working as clearly as if the mental gears were visible. She was building up a picture, a romantic, Hollywood-inspired version of selfless patriotic soldiers gathering for a heroic clandestine rescue operation. The truth was, it hadn't been anything like that at all—some of the things they'd seen and done were the sort of things they hadn't wanted to talk about even among themselves. He knew he'd better put a stop to her imaginings before she had him slated for the role of hero.

"All right, yes," he admitted. "I was in the military. The Special Forces. Dobbs was one of my men. And no, I can't talk about it even if I wanted to, which I don't. Are you satisfied?"

Leaning back, she folded her arms and studied him, her eyes growing concerned. "What's wrong with you, Murdock? Why are you so upset?"

"*Upset?*" He practically spat the word. "I'm not upset. I don't get *upset.*"

"Well, something's causing you a great deal of internalized, unconscious anger," she said, waving her fingers close to her own lips, "because you're getting very white around your mouth and you're breathing pretty fast."

Gripping the steering wheel even tighter, Murdock shook his head in vexation and took a corner at top speed. "My God," he cursed hoarsely to himself. "Why me?"

"Why you what?"

He glared at her and had to swerve to avoid a pedestrian. "Of all the P.I.s in this city, why'd you have to latch on to me? I swear to God, you're enough to drive a sane man 'round the bend."

She blinked at him, a wounded look on her face that made him grit his teeth. "That's not a very nice thing to say."

Braking at a light, he stared sullenly ahead.

"You can't just go around saying things like that," she went on. "You might hurt other people's feelings. I think you should apologize."

He gave her a quick scowl of disbelief. "Apologize?"

"Yes, you know. Say you're sorry."

"Say I'm . . . For what?" he demanded.

"For being so grouchy and mean all morning."

"Grouchy and . . . I am not grouchy and mean, and I am *not* going to apologize. Grouchy and mean," he repeated irritably. Was he?

Raising her eyebrows, she gave him a deliberate, searching look, tinged with the mildest suggestion of disappointment. He'd seen that look before when he was a kid in Catholic school. The nuns had it down to a fine art.

"That's a good one," he said, accelerating again as the light turned green. "You've been pestering me from the second we met, and *I'm* supposed to say I'm sorry."

Her eyes widened. "I have been?"

Without replying, he turned the wheel and headed down the street toward the address she'd given him. Was he really as bad as she said? Probably, he admitted. He'd been ill-tempered all his life. Well, he wasn't about to start apologizing for it now. If she thought he was mean, she could just stop meddling in his life and save them both a lot of trouble.

"But I thought we were working together pretty well," she said, a puzzled note in her voice.

"Working together?" He gave a short, rough laugh. With a squeal of the brakes, he pulled up outside the squat, redbrick medical center. "You must be joking. We aren't working together. We've *never* worked together. I promised to do you one favor, remember? Well, I've done it. We talked to Dobbs, and there's nothing in it. So, now you're on your own." He waved at the passenger door. "Goodbye."

"Goodbye?" She stared at him. "But didn't you hear what Sergeant Dobbs said? He thinks Howard Kavin didn't have a family. But I know he did."

"No, you don't. All you know is that Kavin *told* you he had a family."

"But why would he do that? Why would he lie?"

"Who knows? The point is, there's nothing in it. Kavin got drunk and fell in the river. Period. End of story.

Now, if you don't mind, I've got work to do. I've got a client, too, remember?"

"You're going to see your client?"

His sigh was more like a huff of frustration. "Yes. I am." He wasn't meeting with Erskine Greenwood for several hours, but he wasn't about to let her know that.

"Without me?"

"Of course, without you," he snapped, barely contained exasperation making his voice even hoarser than usual.

"And that's it?" She blinked at him, a tiny furrow appearing between her eyes. "You're just going to drive away?"

Damn, she was good, Murdock told himself. The small catch in her voice was a clever touch, and giving him that baffled hurt look was as sneaky a way of getting under his skin as any he'd known. Then he sighed with defeat. There was no way he could convince himself that she was acting, and *that* was really what made her so good.

"Let me go with you," she asked, leaning toward him and reaching for his arm in appeal. "Can't you wait for me? I won't be long. Barely an hour. Please, take me with you. I promise I won't be in the way. I won't say a word. Just give me a chance to find out what happened to Howard Kavin. This case... it's everything to me, Murdock. Maybe my whole career as a private eye. If your client knows anything about—"

"No."

Above the crook of his arm, her slim, white hand rested as lightly as a feather. And yet she might have been clutching his arm in a vise grip, so powerful was the sensation of her touch.

The jolt ripped through his sinews and bones right down to his gut.

The unexpected depth of his reaction to her touch, like a violent quake tearing through to his soul, staggered him. Savagely, even more roughly than he'd intended, he jerked his arm away.

In his confusion and alarm, his voice was almost a snarl. "Go on and get out of here. I don't want anything more to do with you. Understand?"

Her green eyes widened, growing as misty as the sea in a dawn fog. Speechlessly, she stared at him.

"Don't bother me anymore," he added just as harshly.

"All right," she answered hollowly. Her eyes searched his, even as she reached behind her for the door handle. "If that's what you want."

He didn't reply.

She pushed open the door, but instead of getting out, she paused to contemplate him. "I just want to know one thing. Why did you do it? If this is how you feel, why did you kiss me . . . like that . . . this morning?"

It was cruel, he knew, even as he turned to gaze coldly at her. But he felt cruel. The enormity of his reaction to her demanded ruthlessness. Necessitated brutality.

Callously he formed the words, "Why not?"

He heard the sharp intake of her breath, saw her cheeks drain of color, and then she was gone. In a flustered flurry, she'd jumped from the car, leaving behind only the echo of the slamming door to ring in his ears.

As SHE WAITED for the doctor, Georgie sat on the edge of a paper-covered examining table, trying to hold together both her temper and the flimsy paper gown. She wasn't very successful at either. As for the pool of misery that had begun to fill the empty hole in the pit of her stomach, well, that was something she wasn't going to permit herself to think about just yet.

For a brief moment in the elevator on the way up to Dr. Knapp's office, she'd almost started to cry. Luckily, she'd caught herself in time. Later tonight, when she was alone in bed and couldn't avoid it, then maybe she'd let the tears come. But right now, it was easier to be angry.

And there was no one she was angrier with than herself. Oh, how could she have been so stupid? She thought she'd learned her lesson with Stuart the Rat Lice. Clearly, she didn't have good luck with men. Hadn't she made up her mind to avoid wading into that kind of mess again? So what was wrong with her? Did she have a sign on her forehead that read Use Me, I'm Gullible, or something?

That was the real problem. She *was* gullible. With Stuart it had been different. Somehow, deep inside her, she'd known all along that he wasn't the sensitive, caring man he made himself out to be. If it hadn't been for the hordes of students who'd adored him, she might have trusted her own instincts much sooner.

But with Murdock she hadn't felt that uneasy distrust—that niggling sense that under the personable exterior might beat a less than admirable heart. If anything, she'd felt the opposite. There was nothing slick or winning about Murdock's exterior. He was as prickly as a hedgehog and as gruff as an irritated grizzly. Yet she had thought she'd caught a glimpse of something solid and good, something honest and incorruptible in him.

Well, she'd been wrong, which should come as no great surprise. She'd been wrong before. She just didn't think she'd ever been fooled so completely. In an amazingly short time and despite all his faults, she'd come to trust and like Murdock—never mind what being near him did to her insides. Now she realized what a fool she'd been.

It was a good thing she'd learned in time, Georgie told herself, before they spent many more hours together. Before there were any more kisses that took her breath away and stole her sanity. Thank goodness, she thought, she'd never see him again.

The misery rose a little higher in her, threatening to spill over, and Georgie swallowed hard against the tears that sprang to her eyes. Clutching the edge of the examining table, she took a long, deep breath to steady herself, just as the door opened.

Dr. Knapp poked a pink balding head around the doorway. "Hello, Georgie. How are you feeling?"

Letting out her breath, Georgie nodded. "All right, I guess. I've just been a little stressed lately. That's all. But you know what my mom's like. Apparently, stress wasn't around when she was growing up, so it doesn't really exist. It's nothing, really. . ."

FIVE BLOCKS FROM Jimmy Ray Thompson's apartment, Murdock suddenly gave the Buick's steering wheel a vicious yank and brought the car to an abrupt stop beside the curb. For a long while he sat completely still and stared blindly out the smeared glass of the windshield. Beneath the crumpled felt hat pulled low over his eyes, his face was hard and strained.

Once again Georgie's face rose before him, wan and naked with surprise and undisguised hurt. Briefly, he closed his eyes against the image. Had it really been necessary to be so brutal?

With his hands gripped around the steering wheel, Murdock clenched his teeth and exhaled sharply. Yes, he answered. Yes, it had been the only way.

The residential street was quiet and peaceful, sleepy in the Saturday-afternoon sun. But for Murdock, the silence inside the car was oppressive. The seat beside him was empty, and there was no more endless chatter, no more gestures of boundless energy and no more brilliant smiles that included him in their radiance. There was only him, sitting alone in a battered, aging car on a street that wasn't his own.

That was the way it had always been. That was the only way it could be. He'd *had* to be cruel, he reminded himself. For her sake, he'd had to repulse her — and repulse her so thoroughly she'd never think of seeing him again. Of caring for him. Of responding to his kiss with such sweet abandonment.

He'd done it to save her, he nearly protested aloud. Yet, in the deadly quiet of the car, his next thought, unbidden and unwanted, was as deafening as thunder — *he'd done it to save himself.*

Stunned, Murdock gazed blankly at the street before him. The heavy silence in the car pressed down on him so that each breath he took was an effort, and its loud emptiness rang in his ears. Before he could stop himself, the rush of memories swept over him, turbulent and violently vivid.

"You only think of *yourself*." A woman's voice, strident and acrimonious, was raised in anger. "You don't care about us. You never have. So busy with your war games. So busy satisfying your own needs. You've never thought about us."

Black eyes flashed in accusation and bitterness, and there was the faint, familiar smell of gin on her breath.

"Where are you going?" he asked, stepping forward. Both mother and daughter shrank from him. From *him*. "Where are you taking her?"

"What do you care? You've never been here for us before. What do you care where we go or what we do? We're nothing to you. Nothing."

Another pair of black eyes, timid and frightened, gazed at him from behind her mother's back.

"Isabel," he warned. "Please. Not in front of the child."

"Her *name* is Kristen. And there's no reason to pretend to shield her. She knows. She knows everything. She knows you couldn't even be there when she was born."

He started to explain. "That's unfair. I wanted to be here. You know I did. We were in South America. There was no way I could get back in—"

But of course, she hadn't wanted to hear. Not then. Not any longer.

"You always have an excuse. That's the one thing you've always been able to give us. Excuses for why you can't be a husband. Excuses for why you can't be a father. Well, I'm saving you the trouble of having to come up with any more excuses."

Still hiding behind her mother, the little girl began to whimper soundlessly. His little girl. His Kristen.

"You're upsetting her," he said. "Don't do this now. Not in front of Kristen. Can't this wait for a better time?"

"There won't be a better time. There isn't going be any other time at all. Because I'm leaving you, and I'm taking Kristen with me. Tonight."

"Isabel—"

"You won't have to worry about us ever again. If you ever did." Her eyes narrowed venomously. "You won't have to worry about being here for birthdays or school plays. You won't have to worry about being here for another child's birth."

Incredibly, horribly, he felt his lips begin to turn in a surprised smile. "Another child? You mean—"

"I aborted it." She *did* smile then, and there was something spiteful in that smile and something else. Something like triumph. "You don't deserve to be a father. I won't let you do to another child what you've done to Kristen."

He stood in the center of the kitchen, his hands hanging like dead weights at his sides. Never before had he felt such a rush of anger, a rage more blinding than the blackest night.

"A child," he somehow managed to say. "*My* child."

"*Not anymore.*"

He stood there with his eyes closed, still and completely unmoving, and he let them leave. He heard the door slam as they walked into that snowy winter night, and he let them go.

There was nothing else he could do. For the first time in his life he realized how intensely he could hate. And so he stood without stirring, afraid that if he made the slightest move, if he opened his eyes even a crack, the spell might be over and he might just murder Isabel.

When the police came just before dawn, they found him sitting awake in the cold, dark living room, an empty bottle of whiskey on the floor beside him. They tried to explain to him what had happened, but he already knew from the looks on their faces. They tried to tell him about the accident, but a mysterious deafness seemed to have come over him. Shutting him off from everything and everyone around him.

He knew in that instant that he would live with the black rage for the rest of his life. In that moment, he realized what he'd done by not stopping Isabel . . .

Not that Isabel wasn't right. He *was* a lousy husband and a worse father. Everything she'd accused him of was true. He didn't deserve a family.

Yet he'd had one, anyway. He'd had two children, and they were both gone and there was nothing left anymore but the rage.

His hands on the steering wheel were white-knuckled, and Murdock squeezed his eyes shut, resting his forehead between his fists. How long had he lived with the guilt? Five years? Six? Too long, at any rate, to change now.

Not that he'd ever really tried. That spring, he'd left the military, come home and started the P.I. agency. But it had been an empty gesture. Isabel had already moved to Florida, and it was too late for Kristen. By that time it had been too late for him, as well.

On that bitterly cold February night, he'd been cut off from the ordinary world and the rest of humanity. Nothing could ever change that, and he knew it. And so he'd learned to live in the dead silence of his exile.

That is, he had until a few short days ago.

Raising his head from the steering wheel, Murdock turned again to gaze at the empty seat beside him. She had blown into his life like a fresh, sun-warmed breeze warming a . . . a cold musty tomb.

He paused. Yes, a tomb, he repeated to himself. His life had become a tomb. *And let the dead,* he quoted unexpectedly, *bury the dead.*

With sudden decision, he started the car and pulled out into the street toward Jimmy Ray's. If he'd been cruel to her, well, she'd get over it, he told himself, pausing at a stop sign. And if she pursued the case, which he was almost willing to bet on, then that was her business. If she got into trouble, she could always go to her uncle. She didn't need him.

No, he repeated emphatically, she certainly didn't need him. *He* was the last thing a woman like Georgie needed.

Of course, he continued, it *was* her case and she had a right to any information he might dig up. Not that there would be any information, he hastily amended. But if there was, well, he could always send her a report.

There was no reason for him to go back to the medical center and wait for her. In fact, he insisted adamantly, there was every reason in the world for him to stay away.

Several blocks from Jimmy Ray's, Murdock could make out Reilly sitting on a stoop across the street. In a ragged coat and laceless sneakers, his sometime "assistant"—a generous word—appeared to be sound asleep. With help like Reilly, Murdock told himself, he didn't have time to waste placating some woman. No, there was nothing on earth that could induce him to go back for her.

And yet, when he turned the Buick around sharply, a block from Jimmy Ray's, and accelerated back down the quiet street, he wasn't surprised. He was making the worst mistake of his life, Murdock acknowledged. But he was going back for her, anyway.

Somehow, despite everything he'd told himself, he'd known all along that he would.

GEORGIE PERCHED on the edge of the examining table and stared at Dr. Knapp in shock.

"Could you—" Her voice came out high and squeaky, and she gulped nervously. "Could you repeat that?"

"Certainly. I said you might be experiencing some stress, but that isn't the principle cause of your symptoms."

Georgie fluttered her hands vaguely. "No, not that part. The other thing."

"Oh, of course." Dr. Knapp clasped his hands in front of his belly, eager to oblige. "You're pregnant. Almost two months, I'd say."

5

GEORGIE CROSSED the wide, marble entry of the medical center, not sure what she was thinking or even if she was capable of any thought at all. She felt only a strange, awestruck calm—and a dazed sense of incomprehension.

Standing before the glass doors to the street, she paused and laid her hand on her flat stomach. A baby, she repeated to herself for the twentieth time. She was going to have a baby.

As though she were sleepwalking, Georgie pushed through the glass doors, awkwardly clasping her purse with all the pamphlets and vitamins and appointment schedules the nurse had thrust at her. In a stupor, she headed down the steps.

The voice shouted three times before she realized it was her name being called. She slowly turned and saw Murdock standing beside the old Buick, his hand on the hood and his hat pushed back on his head. She gazed blankly at him. Vaguely she took in the odd expression on his face. His wide, sensuous mouth was pressed in a resentful line, yet his gray eyes were fixed on her with something that looked like apprehension.

For a long moment, she peered at him in confusion, too shaken by her recent discovery to fully register his presence.

"Well?" he asked ungraciously. "Are you coming or not?"

"Murdock?" Her frown was puzzled. "What are you doing here?"

With an impatient lift of his shoulder, he scowled at the building, at the street, at the sky, then at the car. "We're going to be late," he said brusquely, not answering her. "You better get a move on."

"Late?"

"Yes, *late*." He finally met her eyes. "For the meeting. Remember?"

"No, I don't think so. What meeting?"

He tilted his head, squinting at her from under the brim of his hat. "Are you okay?"

A sudden rush of panic swept through Georgie at his words. My God, she thought a little wildly. She was going to have a baby.

"Georgie?" He took a step toward her, thrusting a thumb in the direction of the medical center. "What happened? You get some bad news or something? I mean, you're okay, aren't you?"

A *baby*. It felt as though she couldn't breathe, and for a second Georgie thought she might begin laughing . . . or crying. She wanted to dance, singing, down the street. She wanted to sink to the stairs behind her and weep.

He took another step toward her, and now she could see he was truly worried. "Georgie?"

She wrapped her arms around her purse, clutching it to herself for support. "I'm fine," she said quickly. Too quickly. "Really. I'm okay. I just can't go with you now, Murdock. Maybe another time."

"Another time? What are you talking about?"

"I'm going to catch a cab," she said, turning zombie-like toward the sidewalk.

"Wait a minute. A cab? Where are you going? What about the meeting? I thought you wanted to grill my client about Howard Kavin."

A baby, Georgie thought again, pausing in renewed astonishment. At this very moment, a whole, brand-new life was budding inside her. Right at this moment.

"Georgie!"

Absently, she looked back at him. "Thanks for waiting for me. I'll see you later."

"Waiting for you? I wasn't wait—" He pulled at his hat. "You're still mad at me."

She studied him vacantly. "I am? Why would I be— Oh! *Mad* at you. No. No, I'm not mad at you. At least, not anymore."

"But you don't want to come with me."

"No." She drew the word out. "I have to go home now."

"You *are* mad." He grimaced and averted his face. The square line of his jaw worked silently. Without turning back to her, he muttered, "I'm sorry."

Georgie squinted. "What?"

Clearing his throat noisily, he rapped the hood of the car with his knuckles and nodded mysteriously to himself several times. "I said," he growled a bit fiercely, "that I'm sorry."

"For what?"

"For—" Now he did look at her. "All right, if that's how you want to play it. I'm sorry for being such a damned bast—er, jerk. I'm sorry I said those things to you. Now, will you get in the damned car?"

His look was so anxious there was only one thing Georgie could do in her present state of mind.

"Sure," she said, shrugging, and let him open her door. "Could you drop me at my place?"

"At your . . . ?" Shaking his head, he raised his hands in the air in a gesture of hopelessness as she scooted onto the seat.

"Right," he muttered under his breath. "Now you want to go home. Okay. I give up. *I'm* not going to ask."

IN THE BAR of the Landis Hotel, Murdock sat in an uncomfortably stiff, fake-leather chair and watched Erskine Greenwood across the low, round cocktail table that was barely large enough to hold their two glasses of beer and the ashtray where the butt of Greenwood's third cigarette smoldered. He was talking again, Murdock vaguely realized. The man didn't seem able to shut up. Yet, although Murdock's eyes never left Greenwood's face, his mind was not on his client's words.

All the way to Georgie's apartment, she'd sat quietly beside him, gazing out the window as if her thoughts were a million miles away. He couldn't be sure she wasn't simply ignoring him, paying him back for the way he'd treated her. It was certainly a possibility. But somehow, that explanation didn't ring completely true.

When they reached her building, she'd given him a faint, distracted smile and climbed from the car, barely pausing to thank him for the ride. For a long time, he'd sat outside her apartment and debated whether or not to follow her up and demand to know what was eating her.

In the end, he'd driven away, telling himself that it wasn't his problem. After all, he *had* gone back for her, hadn't he? He'd done more for her than for anyone else in a very long time. If she didn't want anything to do with him, well, it was no skin off his nose. He hadn't wanted her tagging along, anyway.

From across the table, Greenwood's eyes, quick and wary, watched Murdock as he raised his glass and tossed back the remainder of his beer. Tall and lean, with a thin, wispy mustache clipped neat and close, Greenwood seemed to radiate nervous energy. His expensive, somber gray suit hung on him like a costume on a scarecrow. Restlessly, he lit his fourth cigarette in fifteen minutes as he gestured jerkily with his other hand.

"Would you like another one?" Greenwood asked, arranging his cocktail napkin.

"No, I don't want another beer." Murdock's voice was a growl. "I didn't want that one. I'm telling you, Greenwood, you're throwing your money away."

"Really? I'm not sure I agree." His long, skinny fingers fiddled with the cigarette.

Murdock shrugged. "It's your call, but I think it's a waste of time. In the last five days, I've seen enough to convince me, anyhow. Jimmy Ray's not hurting for cash. He's getting it from somewhere." He'd already told Greenwood about the transaction Georgie had spotted in the nightclub. "If I were you, I'd push him for the money he owes you, and I'd do it now. While he still has it."

"Yes, maybe. Maybe." Fretfully, Greenwood pulled at the corner of his little mustache. "But I still think I'd like you to keep an eye on him. Just for a little longer."

Murdock leaned back in his chair and studied Greenwood, his concern for Georgie momentarily overshadowed by sudden suspicion. At their first meeting in the Landis Hotel, Murdock had pegged Greenwood as weak and high-strung, the kind who had too much time and money on his hands. He didn't like Greenwood, but then, if he worked only for clients he liked, he would have gone out of business a long time ago.

Still, the man's story had sounded all right. Jimmy Ray Thompson was the friend of a friend to whom Greenwood had ill-advisedly lent a considerable amount of money. He wanted it back. It was that simple. Not having recourse to the courts because he hadn't asked Jimmy Ray to sign a legal document, Greenwood was forced to turn to other methods.

Jimmy Ray might be stupid, Murdock thought, but that didn't make him a crook. What he wanted, Greenwood had told Murdock, was to know if Jimmy Ray even had enough money to make squeezing it out of him worthwhile. What Greenwood intended to do with that information was something Murdock neither wanted nor cared to know.

Well, he'd done his job, Murdock thought. There was money there, all right, enough money for a top-line Bosch stereo system, alligator-skin boots and a brand-new, shiny Porsche. He didn't need to follow Jimmy Ray to every department store in the city to know the guy had a pile of money and was doing his best to spend it fast.

And yet, why was Greenwood suddenly so anxious to keep him on the job? Something about that didn't set right. In fact, Murdock decided as he watched Greenwood light yet another cigarette from the burning stub of his last, now that he thought about it, Greenwood's edginess was starting to get to him. Just what was the guy so jumpy about?

"I don't know," Murdock said evenly. "I don't like it. I think I'll just send you my bill and say *adios*."

Greenwood's head snapped up. "What? You can't do that. I'm paying you good money for—"

"For information. Which I gave you."

With a tight smile, Greenwood lowered his glass to the table. "You want more money."

"No. I want to know what's going on."

Murdock thought about Georgie and how self-satisfied she'd be if she could hear him now. She'd probably say she told him so. The thought almost made him smile, until he remembered that he wasn't likely to ever see her again.

"Going on?" Greenwood looked surprised. "But I explained all that already. I want the money he owes me. All you have to do is keep an eye on him for just a few more days. Make sure he doesn't leave town. That will give me time to make some plans."

Right, Murdock thought, *and I'm Goldilocks*. With every passing second, he was beginning to distrust Greenwood more and more. That was Georgie's influence, he knew.

Probably he *should* close the file. Send the man a whopping big bill and forget about the case. But if there was one thing he hated, it was being taken for a sucker. If Greenwood was using him, if there was any chance at all that he was connected with Georgie's Howard Kavin, then Murdock knew he wouldn't be able to stop digging. He wasn't about to let this little twerp walk. Not that easily.

"All right," Murdock said, despising the placating tone in his own voice. "If that's all you want. I guess I can stay on the job a few more days."

Greenwood gave a nervous, relieved smile. "Wonderful," he said, rising to his feet. "You'll call me if he makes a move?"

Yeah, I'll call you, Murdock thought. *Just as soon as I get done checking you out—all the way back to kindergarten—which is what I should have done a long time ago.*

"Sure," he said instead. "I'll be in touch."

AT FIRST Stuart Whitmore did not seem to know who she was.

"It's *Georgie*," she repeated reluctantly, hoping the uncertainty in her voice wasn't too apparent. "Georgie Poulopoulos. From your class."

"My class . . . ?" he mused aloud, as though searching for her name.

She knew he was pretending. She supposed it was only natural. After all, he had a wife and three children in California, as she had learned to her horror on that last terrible day. It was in his best interest to have forgotten her name.

When she finally convinced him that he did indeed remember her *and* was going to have to hear her out, he sounded impatient and annoyed but resigned.

"All right. If you insist. But it had better be short," he said irritably. "*And* the last time."

So she told him, flat out and with no preliminaries. Still, his response, so chilly and automatic, took her aback.

"How much do you need?"

"How much what?" Georgie asked.

"Money. I assume that's why you're calling me. I can give you enough to take care of the problem. But don't bother to ask me for any more. That's all I'm giving you. And I'll warn you right now that I can't be threatened."

Perhaps it was his cool, businesslike tone that gave her a clue. Perhaps it was the prompt, ready nature of his offer that told her he'd done this before and had all the angles worked out. Or perhaps it was the personal affront, his insulting assumption that she might try to blackmail him. Too appalled to respond, Georgie merely hung up.

For a long time, she sat cross-legged on the rug, cradling the phone in her lap and biting her lip. Outside the large living-room window, the evening light had turned the sky a dusky purple. She watched the shifting shadows without really seeing them.

Everyone, she reassured herself, was entitled to make a few mistakes in their life. But why did hers have to be so unbelievably brainless? Only complete idiocy could explain why she'd ever gotten involved with Stuart the Rat Lice.

Still, she admitted, she should probably count herself lucky. At least she had a chance to learn from her mistakes. Stuart's wife was doomed to live with hers forever, poor woman.

Georgie sighed. Well, she had done her duty, as distasteful and unpleasant as it had been. Yet despite her relief that it was over, she also felt an unexpected twinge of sadness. She was, Georgie realized, truly on her own now.

Setting aside the phone, she rose slowly to her feet and made her way into the kitchen. Absently, she stood at the sink, then unconsciously raised a hand to her mouth to touch her lips. Yes, she was definitely on her own.

Briefly, Georgie closed her eyes. Oh, sweet Lord, what was she going to do? How was she ever going to cope?

Her dismay swelled as she suddenly remembered her family. What in the world was she going to say to her parents? Never mind their heated theological battles pitting Greek Orthodoxy against the Roman Catholic Church. They were going to be severely scandalized. Her mother would probably stop speaking to her again . . . this time for years.

And what about her job? Georgie thought, clutching the edge of the sink. All her life she'd wanted to be a P.I. She'd worked long and hard to prove herself capable of the job. She couldn't lose her dream now!

Yet how inconspicuous would she be on stakeouts or tailing a suspect as she lumbered along with a huge belly? How could she command an imposing presence in front of criminals with a gurgling baby propped on her hip? If Uncle Nikos had wanted a reason to fire her, she couldn't have handed him a more convenient one.

With tremendous effort, Georgie made herself loosen her grip on the sink. Raising her chin, she inhaled slowly and deliberately. Now was not the time to panic, she told herself sternly. There were too many things to do and too many decisions to be made. Panicking would just have to wait.

Determined to regain a modicum of calm, she twisted the faucet and filled a glass with water. With exaggerated care, she reread the instructions on the bottle of vitamins and measured out three amazingly large pills, swallowing them with a grimace. Then she meticulously rinsed the glass and wandered down the hall to the spare room she'd spent most of her five-year tenancy trying to ignore.

Pausing in the hall, she took another deep breath, then threw open the door. The room was dusty and crammed with boxes. Summer clothes hung in plastic bags, a miscellaneous collection of enthusiastically purchased but little-used exercise equipment huddled in a corner and old skis and tennis rackets were jumbled together with broken appliances and a stack of canvases from the one ill-advised art class she'd taken in her sophomore year. Standing in the doorway she surveyed the disaster, then tentatively, hesitantly, pressed her palm to her stomach.

"All right, kid," she said as cheerfully as she could. "This is it. I hope you like it because it's your room. It doesn't look like much right now, I know, but with a little work, you'll be amazed."

Did she feel a movement? she suddenly wondered with amazement. No, of course not. Dr. Knapp had told her she wouldn't feel anything like that for months. But she'd felt *something*, Georgie knew. She'd felt something powerful and intense and incredibly wondrous stir deep down inside her.

For the first time that evening, her smile was genuine. She wasn't exactly sure how, but she suddenly knew she would make things work. It wasn't going to be easy, but when had she ever refused a good battle? Somehow, someway, she and the little squirt would be okay.

"So," she asked, raising her arms in a wide, expansive gesture, "what color do you want the walls?"

DOWN THE STREET from Eddie's Tavern, Murdock pushed open the door of the Buick and climbed slowly, wearily, from the car. Miraculously, Reilly had shown up at Jimmy Ray's—for once before the bars closed. He was drunk anyway, of course, but the bottle he'd brought with him would probably last him a few hours, long enough for Murdock to shower and catch a few winks.

He probably should have come straight home, Murdock told himself, using the short time for sleep to its fullest advantage. But tonight he'd taken a different route back to Eddie's. Tonight he'd somehow ended up in front of a gracefully aging building shadowed by large trees just beginning to bud.

Tonight he'd found himself parked across the street, staring up at the dark windows in a third-story, corner apartment and wishing the lights were on. Her windows, of course, had stayed dark. And so he'd finally started the car and driven home.

With his hands in his pockets, Murdock headed down the sidewalk toward Eddie's, passing the rows of silent, dark cars parked along the curb. It was near closing time, and he saw a group swing out of the front doors of the tavern several blocks away. Just ahead of him a couple strolled down the sidewalk, arms twined around each other as they laughed uproariously, so engrossed in one another they barely glanced at him.

Stepping off the sidewalk, he let them pass and watched as they disappeared down the street. Even after they turned the corner, he continued to gaze into the empty night, until gradually he became aware of the blue, flickering light of a television in the front window of the house across the street. As he watched, a man rose to his feet, his shadow dark against the curtained window. The man bent down and, the next instant, reappeared with the shape of a sleeping child in his arms.

Strangely unable to look away, Murdock stared at the window as a slighter, shorter shadow joined the first, merging with the man's as they embraced. Then one of them reached out, and the ghostly blue glow was snuffed out.

For a long while, Murdock stood on the sidewalk, watching the blank window, listening to the laughter from the group in front of Eddie's, and barely noticing that his hands were clenched in fists at his sides. The urge to howl—to raise his face and bellow at the sickle-shaped moon like some mangy, starving stray—was almost overwhelming. Just when he thought he could stand it no more, he finally forced himself to break away and head home.

In the smoky, crowded bar, he shouldered his way through to the hall at the back, stripped off his clothes in the room upstairs and let them drop unheeded to the floor. Between limp, creased sheets, he lay very still and straight in bed and gazed up at the ceiling, watching the reflection from the colorful beer lights hung in the windows downstairs and listening to the happy, boisterous noise of the crowd below.

Long after the last burst of laughter and shouted goodbyes had died away, long after the last flicker of passing headlights crossed the ceiling, he lay there, unsleeping and unmoving, while odd fragments of half-remembered nursery rhymes ran in a ceaseless singsong through his head.

This is the house that Jack built. This is the house that Jack built. This is the house he built. And the walls came tumbling down.

When the shrill ring of the phone tore the silence of the night, he leaned over and lifted the receiver with relief.

IN AN UNUSUAL BURST of energy, Georgie woke at seven the next morning and, wide-awake anyway, decided there was no time like the present to deal with the dreaded task. Not even the regrettably familiar nausea that had her moaning in the bathroom could daunt her spirits.

By noon she'd already made a good start on the spare room. Dressed in sweatpants and a baggy T-shirt, carrying a large, overflowing cardboard box balanced awkwardly in her arms, she struggled to twist the knob of the apartment's front door. The box began to topple to one side, and she made a grab for it just as the door swung open.

"Ah!" Georgie squealed. The box hit the floor with a loud thud.

Standing in the hallway with his hand still raised, Murdock stepped back, as surprised as she was.

"Murdock?" she gasped in disbelief. "What on earth are you doing here?"

With a vaguely puzzled expression, he gazed down at the battered lamp shade and ancient toaster, old notebooks and magazines, worn sneakers and mismatched socks that spilled from the box. In the dim light of the hall, his rugged face was all shadows and planes . . . and disarmingly handsome.

Once again he wore the black leather jacket, but instead of baggy khakis, a pair of stylishly faded, obviously new jeans rode low on his hips. His white shirt was wrinkled, as usual, except for the stiffly smooth collar and an uncreased patch around the pocket, which puzzled Georgie until she realized he must have made an attempt to iron his shirt. For Murdock, she guessed, this was dressing up, and she couldn't help wondering why he'd taken the trouble.

Ruefully, Georgie glanced down at her own dusty T-shirt and sweatpants. Why hadn't she worn something nicer to clean out the spare room—like black chiffon and high heels?

"I didn't know if you'd be here," he said, bending down to help her gather the stuff together. Their hands brushed, and she saw him swallow. "I mean, on a Sunday afternoon."

Squatting just inside the door and holding a broken curling iron in her hand, she tilted her head to the side quizzically. She tried to suppress the rush of joy she felt at the sight of him, but it was no use. Georgie grinned, unable to stop herself. He'd come back, she thought with irrepressible joy. She shouldn't be happy. She shouldn't feel glad. But she did. Oh, she did.

"That's why you're here? Because you didn't think I would be?"

"Well, no." He reached for two badly singed pieces of quilted cloth shaped like parrots. "I mean, I hoped you would be home. I got a call late last night from—"

Breaking off, he looked at the scorched parrots. "What *are* these things?"

"They're hot pads," she said, taking them from him and tossing them into the box. "I was trying to make cookies one day, and I must have left them in the oven too long."

"Oh, I see." He didn't look as if he saw at all.

In the act of rising, he glanced through the open door at the chaos in the living room and halted sharply. Was she imagining it or did his face pale just the tiniest bit?

"You're moving?" he asked, staring at the room.

"What? Oh, no. I'm just cleaning out a spare bedroom. Sort of a junk room."

She could have sworn he looked relieved.

"There sure is a lot of junk," he said, stepping into the apartment with her and scanning the disorder. His boots sounded heavy on the wooden floor as he turned, and Georgie noticed they'd been polished. "Is it all yours?"

"All mine, I'm afraid," she answered lightly, biting her lip to keep the silly grin off her face. "I can't stand throwing anything out. The second you do, you always discover you need that one particular thing. Even if you haven't used it in years."

"I throw everything out," he said, prodding a crippled lawn chair with his toe.

"Somehow, Murdock, that doesn't surprise me."

Perching on the edge of the sofa, Georgie unclipped the barrette holding back her hair and ran her fingers through it, trying to collect her confused thoughts. For a start, she wished she didn't feel like throwing her arms around him. If she had any sense, she would ask him to leave. Hadn't he made it perfectly plain that he neither liked nor approved of her? Where was her pride?

And yet she couldn't deny her happiness at seeing him. Perhaps, Georgie thought, this lunacy was just another of the weird symptoms of pregnancy. It had to be some kind of craziness because, from the instant she'd met Murdock, hadn't she felt drawn to him like a bee to honey?

It certainly wasn't his charming personality that attracted her. He was curt and cross, thorny as a cactus, and to top it off, he'd hurt her feelings. He had every characteristic of the classic misanthrope. So why did she sense that, under that grumpy exterior, there was kindness in him?

Struck by a thought, Georgie sat up straighter. It had to be a mask—a pretense to prevent anyone's getting too close to him. That could explain why he'd come back for her yesterday, why he was here today and why he'd ever agreed to help her in the first place. Not that it was *all* an act—he was far too grouchy for that. But maybe parts of it weren't quite as real as he . . .

"What?" Murdock demanded, his hands raised palms up. He glanced down uneasily at himself. "What's wrong?"

"Wrong?" Georgie asked, a little dazed by her unexpected revelation.

"Yeah. You were staring at me."

"No, I wasn't."

"Yeah, well, cut it out, anyway."

A sudden smile split Georgie's face. Oh, yes, she thought with just the slightest hint of satisfaction. She was beginning to understand Mr. Tough-Guy Murdock.

Raising her arms over her head, she stretched happily, lifted her hair off her neck and pinned it back with the barrette. Unable to resist, she said, raising her eyebrows a fraction, "You combed your hair."

With a jerk, his hand moved toward his head, then dropped. Massive, leather-clad shoulders lifted in a disinterested shrug that didn't fool her one bit.

"Yeah? So? Sometimes I do that," he said. Turning, he pretended to study a Van Gogh print hung over a bookcase.

"And shaved," Georgie relentlessly continued.

When he looked at her, his eyes were narrowed as though he suspected her of teasing him. But his response was touchingly serious, almost apologetic. "I always do. It just, well, it grows fast."

As if he'd just disclosed some shockingly intimate secret about himself and could hardly believe his own ears, he frowned darkly, his discomfort telling Georgie more clearly than anything how unused he was to revealing himself to another person.

He squared his shoulders and, assuming a stern expression, attempted to regain control of the conversation. Taking pity on him, Georgie let him.

"I came over here this morning for a reason."

"Of course," she agreed, not smiling.

He shot her another quick look, but when she returned it steadily, he merely scowled and went on.

"Dobbs called me last night. Said he'd been thinking about the case."

Case? Georgie wondered, deciding the intense, almost haunted look in Murdock's gray eyes was one of his most intriguing characteristics. What case? Oh! she thought suddenly. *That* case.

"I guess we put a bee in his bonnet about Jimmy Ray Thompson," Murdock was saying. "He started digging around after he got back to the station. Trust Dobbs. He never forgets a name."

Georgie blinked at him. "Sergeant Dobbs remembered something? What was it?"

"It seems our Jimmy Ray has done a considerable amount of time, on and off, in the slammer. Mostly for grand larceny. His last government-sponsored vacation was in the pen at Joliet for—" here, Murdock paused for dramatic effect, which had Georgie dangerously on the edge of her seat "—the Meckelmann job."

She crossed her arms, gave a soundless whistle and tried to look intelligent. "No! Really?"

Murdock shook his head sadly. "Unbelievable, huh?"

"It sure is," Georgie agreed heartily as she scoured her brain and still came up blank.

"I'll admit it made me feel like a real idiot."

"Oh, I know," she commiserated, nodding just as sadly. "I know what you mean."

What in the world was he talking about? she wondered frantically. She didn't have a clue what the Meckelmann job was.

"So I guess that explains a lot of things," Murdock went on. "When the jewels were never found, everyone assumed that— But you already know all this."

Georgie waved her hand benignly. "Oh, sure. But go ahead and refresh my memory. I might have forgotten a few of the details."

Leaning back against the doorjamb to the kitchen, Murdock crossed his boots at the ankles. "Well, you probably remember that when old man Meckelmann died without any heirs, he willed the entire collection to the Chicago Art Museum. You'd think people would be a little more careful with a collection of priceless jewels like that, wouldn't you?"

"Oh, definitely," Georgie said, realizing her mouth had fallen open.

"Well, maybe it wasn't all their fault," Murdock conceded graciously. "I guess they *did* try to keep things as quiet as possible. Still, the armored transport was held up, anyway, and three men made away with the collection. One of the thieves was found stabbed to death only a few streets away, presumably by his accomplices. Jimmy Ray was picked up a few days later after someone called in an anonymous tip. That's why everyone believed him when he said he didn't know where the jewels were."

"I don't get it," Georgie said, forgetting that she was supposed to know all about the case. "What made them so sure he was telling the truth?"

"Because someone had turned him in. It seemed obvious that the third man had the jewels and was doing away with his partners so he could keep the whole take himself. He was the real leader. Everyone thought Jimmy Ray was just a stooge. When Jimmy Ray refused to name his accomplice, that seemed to cinch matters. Obviously, he was terrified enough of this guy to take the whole rap himself. He got three years in the slammer for his trouble, anyhow."

Georgie stared thoughtfully at Murdock, her forehead creased. "You believe," she said slowly, "that Jimmy Ray might have known where the jewels were all along. That *he* was the one who hid them."

Murdock's lips curled in that slow, dangerous smile she was beginning to recognize. "No, I don't think so. I *know* so. Did you see those alligator boots? That silver Porsche? No con fresh out of the pen can afford stuff like that. Not unless he has a stash waiting for him. And another thing, if the third partner had the jewels, why haven't any of them turned up?"

"Do you think Howard Kavin knew all this?"

"It seems likely."

"And your client?"

Murdock grimaced. "I don't usually divulge information about my clients, but yes, I'm starting to have my suspicions about Greenwood. He says he just wants to recover a personal loan. But unless he loaned Jimmy Ray money in the slammer, Greenwood's timing is seriously off. Jimmy Ray hasn't been out that long."

Georgie gnawed the tip of her thumb, turning over all the information in her mind. Finally, she glanced up at Murdock. "So, what do we do now?"

For a long moment, their gazes met and held, Georgie's green eyes a little apprehensive, Murdock's gray eyes cool and emotionless. The "we" in her question hung in the air between them, so laden with meaning it was almost visible.

Just when she thought the tension had reached the breaking point, she saw a muscle twitch in Murdock's jaw. Then he pushed himself away from the doorjamb.

"Dobbs gave me the name of Jimmy Ray's cellmate in the pen," he said slowly, significantly. "His name's Walters. I know him. Not well. But he might talk to us."

Georgie let out her breath before she'd even realized she'd been holding it. "You mean, both of us? You want us to work together?"

Murdock's frown turned fierce, and he jammed his hands into the pockets of his leather jacket. For a second, she thought he might be about to tell her to take a hike. Instead, he cleared his throat.

"It's your case," he said with sudden vigor. "You were the one who said something was going on. You were the one who was right. God knows, I don't put up with anyone crowding me, and I guess I don't expect you to feel any different."

"So you're going to help?"

His expression was reluctant, but he nodded, anyway. "Yeah. I'll help. But only under one condition. No matter what we turn up, you don't go off on any hare-brained sleuthing missions by yourself."

Georgie opened her mouth, about to protest, but he held up a hand.

"That's the deal," he said, and his tone was uncompromising. "Take it or leave it. This isn't the kind of case you can afford to make mistakes with. Not when one man's already been stabbed to death and another is lying in the morgue with his lungs full of river water."

Georgie felt her face pale. "So you believe me about Howard Kavin? You think he was murdered, too?"

"I don't think anything. Except that there are already two corpses and three probably won't upset anybody too much. If you want my help on this, you have to listen to me." He paused as though for emphasis. "Don't forget, there's still an unknown element out there."

"A what?"

"The third jewel thief. The one no one ever caught. The one who doesn't have a name. Chances are he's still out there. And my bet is he's pretty damned ticked off."

6

"THERE'S ALWAYS the chance that Howard Kavin was the third thief," Murdock said as he pulled the Buick away from the takeout window of the fast-food restaurant. "Kavin could have been waiting for Jimmy Ray to get out, and when Kavin approached him, Jimmy Ray killed him so he wouldn't have to share the jewels."

Beside him, Georgie was hungrily devouring a hamburger as though she hadn't eaten in a week. Fascinated despite himself, Murdock watched her swallow a fistful of french fries.

"No, I don't think so," she said around a mouthful, shaking her head. "I can't believe that— My word, this is good. Are you sure you don't want some?"

It was obvious she was famished. When he shook his head, she looked relieved although she tried to hide it. With renewed gusto, she dug into a second burger, talking between bites.

"No. No, Howard Kavin was too timid to be involved in a daring jewel heist," she said, sipping her soda through a straw. "He wasn't the type."

Murdock's quick laugh was cynical. "Oh, yeah? And what type is that? Take my word for it, most of humanity won't stop at much. At least not when that kind of money is involved."

"Not Howard." She shook her head. "He was an introvert with an anxiety complex and clear repressive traits."

"He was a *what?*"

They'd been passing row after row of small, run-down houses on their way to Walters's place. The curbs were lined with skeletons of disabled, burned-out cars and the lawns looked neglected and weed-choked. He waved his hand at the window.

"Look, you don't know these streets like I do. Half these people would do in their best friend for a buck. I'm telling you, all the fancy words in the world won't help you out here. The only way to survive is to be quicker, stronger and meaner than they are."

She ate a french fry, studying him thoughtfully. "Howard Kavin wasn't a jewel thief."

"Well, he knew something." Murdock glanced at the address on the scrap of paper in his hand. "Because he is definitely dead."

"Maybe he just heard something about the jewels and put two and two— Oh, drat!"

Murdock stopped peering at the house numbers for a moment and glanced over at her. She was pawing through the fast-food bag as though she suspected the jewels were in there.

"Look at this," she wailed, holding up a plastic container of ice cream. "I asked for caramel topping. Didn't you hear me ask for caramel?"

He shrugged uncertainly, bewildered at the quick change in conversation.

"Well, this is *fudge.* They gave me *fudge.*" Even as she complained, she scooped a spoonful into her mouth. "You just can't rely on anyone anymore."

A little mystified, Murdock merely nodded, not about to disagree with her. Neither was he willing to point out that she'd already eaten half the container. He had no idea a young woman of her slender size could put away so much food. Where did she hide it all?

Braking beside the curb, he watched her scrape the container for the last morsel. "We're here," he announced. "Maybe you'd better come in with me. I don't want you to start gnawing on the upholstery or anything."

She gave him a lopsided smile. "I *was* pretty hungry," she agreed, pushing open her door. "It's the strangest thing, but lately I've been either starving or—"

On the sidewalk she stopped abruptly and a pink flush crept up her cheeks. In her cherry-red blazer, formfitting jeans and with her shiny dark hair spilling over her shoulders, she looked out of place in the squalid, littered street, like a new copper penny glinting brightly in the dark gutter.

If he had any sense at all, Murdock told himself, he'd drive her straight out of this seedy neighborhood and away from the whole sordid case. The schoolgirl blush—caused by his comment about her appetite, he guessed—nearly convinced him to bundle her back in the car.

But of course, it wasn't his decision to make. If nothing else, he'd learned that Georgie had a mind of her own. She would fight him tooth and nail. And unlike anyone else he'd ever matched wits with, *she* always seemed to win.

Raising her hand now, she gnawed the tip of her thumb, a gesture of thoughtfulness he was beginning to recognize and find endearing.

"What I meant was," she explained awkwardly, "that I've *always* had a healthy appetite. It's not really anything new or recent . . . or anything."

"Yeah, well, don't worry about it," he said gruffly. "I've known truck drivers who could eat almost as much as you."

She made a face, a funny little grimace, and he heard her murmur, "How comforting," as they headed up the cracked sidewalk.

"By the way," he said, as they climbed the loose, wooden porch steps. "Let me do the talking in there."

"You? But why? That's what I'm good at. Talking to people is my specialty. If you don't mind my saying so, open, sensitive communication is not really your strong suit."

The porch of the little house was buckled with age and neglect, and the whole structure swayed as Murdock crossed to the front door.

"We're not here to analyze the guy," he growled. "We're pumping him for information about his old cellmate. If Jimmy Ray did spill anything to him, he might not feel like sharing. He might need a little persuasion. Leave it to me. Walters knows me. I'll handle things. You just keep quiet for once."

Behind him, he heard her mumble something about obsessive-control complexes as he raised his hand to the door. With his fist still poised in midair, he suddenly felt his heart thud and quicken. Every nerve in his body sprang to life, and his gut turned icy cold. He stood frozen before the door as an eerily familiar sensation crept down his spine. Then instinctively, he reached back, and pulled Georgie close behind him.

She must have sensed his tension because when she spoke, it was in a whisper. "What is it? What's wrong?"

Silently, he shook his head. With quick, alert eyes he scanned the house. Dirty, ragged curtains hung in the grimy windows and there wasn't the slightest sound behind the door. It was quiet. Too quiet. Deathly quiet.

And then he knew. The smell was faint out here on the porch, but he'd lived too long with the cloying, putrid stench of death to ever mistake it.

"Go back to the car," he said, not bothering to whisper. There wasn't any need. There was no breathing, living creature in this house to hear them. Not any longer.

"Go on," he repeated, and tried the door. The knob turned easily.

"But why? What's wrong? I don't want to go back to the car. This is my case, remember? You said so yourself." Stepping forward, she pushed hard on the door with the flat of her hand.

She didn't scream. He had to give her credit for that. With scarcely a gasp, she fell backward against him, turning her face into his chest and whimpering almost soundlessly with her fingers pressed against her mouth.

If he hadn't felt so disconcerted himself, he probably would have bawled her out. Instead, for the second time in as many days, he found his arms around her, cradling her to him.

"All right," he murmured, taking a deep, steadying breath. "It's all right. It's over now."

From somewhere very far away—some dark and murky country he had never thought he'd visit again— words of reassurance rose to his lips. Soothing words, gentle words that he thought he'd forgotten for all time suddenly came to him in an effortless flow as though they'd been on his tongue all the time, only waiting to be spoken.

"It's okay. It's all right now. Come on, sweetheart. Let's go back to the car. That's right. I'm here."

He settled her on the edge of the front seat, crouching beside her in the street. Her face was blanched and her green eyes wide with terror. When she headed for the bushes, he followed her and held her hair until the sickness passed, then he fished out her fast-food cup of soda and watched her drink long and thirstily.

"My God," she finally breathed, her eyes on the house. "Murdock. My God."

And that, he thought to himself, expressed it better than anything. The man inside was barely recognizable as Walters, but that one glimpse had convinced Murdock. Lord only knew how long the poor devil had lain there. If he was any judge—and unfortunately, he was—the man who'd wielded the knife had known exactly what he was doing.

"We're going to have to call the cops," he said, watching her carefully.

"Dobbs," she said shortly.

His smile was quick and surprised. Horrified though she was, the lady didn't let it affect her brains. The grudging respect he'd been harboring for her blossomed a little more.

"Right. We'll call Dobbs. He's not going to be too happy about it. But he'll be less likely to jump to any wrong conclusions about our presence here."

"That man," she said, swallowing hard. "That man in there. He was Walters?"

"Yes."

"He's dead?"

"Very."

"But who—"

"That, Georgie, is what you and I are going to find out."

ORIN DOBBS LET them cool their heels outside Walters's house for nearly three hours as his team went over the house and removed the body. Then he spent another four hours bullying them down at the station. Murdock was right, Georgie discovered. Dobbs wasn't very pleased with them, particularly when Murdock continued to insist that they didn't know anything and Georgie, following his cue, repeated his denials.

It wasn't exactly a lie, either. They *didn't* know anything. They might have a lot of suspicions, but there wasn't one clear piece of evidence in the case. Someone had killed Walters. That was obvious. But if there was any connection between his death, Jimmy Ray, Howard Kavin, Erskine Greenwood and a collection of priceless jewels, it was anyone's guess.

Dobbs was clearly frustrated with them, but long-established respect for his old lieutenant made him keep his temper on a short rein. It was nearly ten at night when he finally yelled at them to get their sorry butts out of his office, but he apparently wasn't going to hold a grudge. As they were leaving, he added, "And get some sleep. You both look like hell."

All the way back to her apartment Georgie huddled in the corner of the car, her arms wrapped around herself in a vain attempt to stop the strange shivering that made her teeth chatter. She had never seen death before—at least not *that* kind of brutal, violent disregard for human life. No matter how she tried, she couldn't erase the bloody scene from her mind.

Certainly the experience couldn't have been good for the baby, she thought anxiously, her arms tightening protectively over her stomach. Didn't they say unborn infants could receive stimuli through the womb?

The poor kid. It had no idea what it was getting into, having her for a parent. Barely a full day of motherhood, and already she'd probably warped her child's psyche for life.

Beside her, Murdock steered the car with sure, expert movements, his profile a mosaic of shadowy angles and chiseled lines in the passing lights of the street. As solid and imperturbable as some ancient Roman statue, he seemed completely untroubled and not at all like a man who had just witnessed the handiwork of a psychotic killer.

In fact, throughout the whole ordeal today, he had remained grim but unflappable, and several times Georgie had felt the urge to reach out and touch him, to cover his large hand with hers and draw comfort and reassurance from his quiet strength.

Of course, she'd done nothing of the kind. That was the very last thing she needed. Murdock already insisted she wasn't cut out to be a detective. She had no intention of giving his arguments any more ammunition by letting him know how upset she was.

No, she could be professional, too. She could be just as cool and dispassionate as he was . . . or, at any rate, she could give her best shot at faking it.

Pulling up outside her building, Murdock turned to her, his gray eyes inscrutable in the shadows. "Will you be all right?"

"Who? Me?" Georgie gave a quick, unconvincing laugh and clenched her teeth so they didn't chatter quite as audibly. "Don't be ridiculous. Why wouldn't I be? This was nothing. All in a day's work, as they say."

"Are you sure?"

"Of course I'm sure," she retorted, unable to resist a quick glance up at the dark windows of her apartment.

She could feel him watching her as she fumbled for the door handle.

"You look a little, well, shaken up," he said.

"Don't be silly. There's nothing wrong with *me*."

"If you want me to go up with you—"

Throwing open her door, she climbed from the car. "Absolutely not. I can manage on my own, thank you very much."

From the corner of her eye, Georgie caught a glimmer of movement under the trees in front of the building, and her heart gave a sickening lurch. Yellow eyes glinted evilly at her out of the night. She nearly squealed aloud when a cat streaked across the yard.

Behind her, Murdock was stepping onto the sidewalk. "I think I'll just walk up with you, anyway."

"Okay."

Wimp, Georgie thought, trying to calm her thudding heart. Was that quick flash of white in the darkness beside her a hastily suppressed smile?

Squaring her shoulders, she marched briskly up the sidewalk and unlocked the front door in a show of steel-nerved bravery. She had half a mind to tell him to go away and stop babying her, she thought as she paused in the foyer and reached for the light. Probably she would have, if she hadn't been so glad to have his large, reassuring presence in the deathly still night.

The foyer was as black as a cave. Georgie turned the switch again. Then once more.

"The light's out," she said calmly enough, though her voice had risen an octave or two. A shiver of fear prickled across her skin.

In the darkness, she heard the creak of Murdock's leather jacket and the scrape of his boots against the floor. The air beside her stirred as he drew near, and

A Toast to Y...
Our Valued
Reader!

EDITOR'S
SWEEPSTAKES
VALIDATION SEAL

A Toast !

Dear Valued Reader,

A "Toast to You" for having chosen
romance novels!

As a part of this special "Toast," and
Editor's $1,000,000.00 Sweepstakes Valid
Validation Seal, once returned by you, wil
personal sweepstakes numbers. These nu
will instantly qualify you for any and all
chance and return your Validation Seal --
numbers is selected in our $1,000,000.0
$1,000,000.00 Winner!

And that's not all...activating your
bring you an elegant long stemmed wine
toasts on those special occasions, and fo
well -- ABSOLUTELY FREE!

So go ahead and place your Editor
spot provided and you can immediately
to You" -- THE OPPORTUNITY TO WIN S

Burgt Davis-Bold   *Paula*

P.S. Validate our Editor's "Toast to You
  PURCHASE NECESSARY -- be in o
  and immediately receive your FRI

With Our Compliments!
The Editors

Your very own set of bookplates to make each Temptation Novel specially yours. Enjoy them with our compliments!

This Book Belongs to:

This Book Belongs to:

This Book Belongs to:

Before sealing, please be sure to...

1. Detach your Editor's Sweepstakes Validation Seal, moisten and place it in the space provided.

2. Fill in your name and address.

3. Detach your Bookplates and make your favorite Temptation Novels personally yours!

suddenly she could feel the heat from his body and smell the faint but unmistakable male scent of his skin, an unfamiliar yet distinctively masculine muskiness as heady as a drug.

Cool, smooth leather brushed her cheek, then rough fingers fumbled over hers, closing over the hand she still had raised to the light switch. At the touch of his skin on hers, his hand paused. She could feel the warmth of his breath on her hair. For a moment, she thought she heard his breath quicken. Or was it hers?

The next instant he dropped his hand.

"It's nothing. Just a burned-out bulb." Despite his words, he spoke in a whisper.

"Yes. That must be it," Georgie said, holding her fingers in the palm of her other hand as though she'd burned them. She wasn't going to panic, she told herself. She was *not* going to make a fool of herself in front of Murdock.

"It's an old building. It must happen a lot."

"Yes," Georgie agreed, barely suppressing the rising note of alarm in her voice. "Light bulbs burn out all the time."

"Still," he said quietly. "Just in case. Do you have a flashlight in your purse?"

"I lost it. Do you have one?"

"In the car."

"Should we get it?"

"Not unless you have some extra batteries."

With a rustle of leather, she heard him move away into the blackness.

"Murdock?"

"Stay here." His deep voice was a low, soft rumble. "I'll be right back."

In the blinding darkness of the foyer, Georgie searched vainly for his shape. Was he moving toward the stairs? A panicked dread of being left behind, helpless and unable to see, swept over her.

"No, wait," she breathed, stumbling forward with her arms outstretched. "I'm coming, too."

"Stay there, I said."

His mistake was in responding. Quickly, she followed the sound of his voice, and nearly toppled them both over onto the stairs when she bumped into him.

"I'm going with you," she whispered, grabbing a handful of the back of his leather jacket.

"For God's sake, Georgie—" He reached behind him to swat her away.

Georgie clung on. "You're not leaving me down here all alone. I won't do it," she insisted, not bothering to sound brave anymore.

"Oh, for the love of— All right, but let go, would you?" he whispered fiercely. "Before I shoot myself. I'm trying to get my gun out, and you're pulling so hard, I can't move my hand."

"What? Oh, sorry." Quickly, she loosened but didn't relinquish her hold on the back of his jacket. They started up the stairs. "What gun? You weren't carrying a gun this afternoon when—"

"Georgie."

"Oh, right. Sorry."

He cautiously crept up the stairs, feeling his way along the wall with Georgie close on his heels. At the first landing he paused, listening, she guessed, then soundlessly started up the next flight of steps.

The third-floor hallway was quiet and still, dimly lit by a small window at the far end. Wordlessly, Murdock motioned her to stay put. When she shook her head furiously, he merely grunted in frustration, raised the hand holding a very efficient-looking 9mm and followed the gun down the wall.

Step by step they inched their way to the door of her apartment, pausing beside it. As they stood there, Georgie pressed her forehead into the smooth, supple leather of Murdock's jacket and felt the strong muscles of his back, hard and taut with tension. Closing her eyes, she tried to fight off the urge to throw her arms around him and pull him back down the corridor to safety.

Slowly, he reached for the knob, then whispered to her, "The key."

"What?"

"The key. It's locked."

"Oh. Oh, right. Just a minute." George swung her purse off her shoulder, balanced it on her knee and rummaged through the accumulated clutter within.

"Come on," he muttered irritably.

"All right, all right. I'm looking. Geez." Pausing abruptly, Georgie glanced once at the ceiling, then pulled a set of keys from the pocket of her jacket.

Like the sound of a grizzly stirring awake in his den, Murdock's grumble was surly, but he took the key from her and soundlessly inserted it into the lock.

"For God's sake, stay out here," he said, the edge in his voice not softened by whispering.

"Do you think the killer—"

"Just stay."

"But—"

"Georgie."

He pushed open the door, paused, then slipped through the opening. Despite his hisses and angry gestures, Georgie followed close behind.

In the pale light from the thin sliver of moon outside the living-room window, the chaotic disorder looked devastatingly complete. Stunned, Georgie halted at the door, surveying the disaster that had been her apartment.

Noiselessly, Murdock crossed to the kitchen, trying lights unsuccessfully as he went. She heard a floorboard squeak in the hall and the faint click of doors opening. When he suddenly reappeared before her, she gave a frightened start.

"No one's here," he said.

Georgie took a faltering step into the room. "My God," she breathed with dismay, throwing out her arms. "Look at this mess. Look what he's done to my home."

Turning slowly, Murdock followed her gaze.

"I can't believe it," she cried. "It's an outrage."

In the darkness, she slipped on a pile of magazines strewn across the floor and stumbled against a low table.

"Georgie."

"This is the work of a seriously disturbed person. Oh, I feel so violated. If I ever get my hands on the guy who—"

"Georgie," Murdock interrupted firmly. "You did it."

Arms raised, Georgie broke off and looked back at him. "Huh?"

"This mess. You did it. This morning, remember? You were cleaning out a spare room."

Frozen with sudden recollection and a horrifying sense of her own stupidity, Georgie gaped at him. Slowly, she lowered her arms.

"Of course," she said quickly. "I can see that."

He seemed about to say something, then changed his mind. Suddenly, he grinned, a wide, brilliantly white smile of irrepressible amusement.

"It's very dark in here," she tried to explain.

His grin widened. Like dusty notes haltingly squeezed from an ancient organ, a short rusty chuckle growled deep in his chest, then another, and another, each coming faster and more insistent than the last until a steady rumble of low male laughter began to echo off the walls.

Georgie eyed him uncertainly, a corner of her mouth involuntarily turning up. Had she ever heard Murdock laugh before?

Standing in the center of the room, his head thrown back and his hands on his hips, he looked large and dark and somehow unreal in the pale glow of the moon. Like some unearthly Nordic god roaring thunderously from his mountaintop, he seemed to dwarf the room, filling it with his mirth.

His laughter was infectious. Despite her chagrin, Georgie gave a reluctant chortle.

"I really did think someone had broken in."

"The look on your face!" He howled, and wiped his eyes.

"It's not *that* funny." She giggled. "I guess I did jump to conclusions a bit."

"A bit?" His laughter deepened. "You were ready to kill someone."

"Yeah, well. What about you? Creeping around with your gun drawn. Just because a few bulbs were burned out."

Taking a step forward, she raised her hand to punch his arm. The scattered pile of glossy magazines were slick under her foot, and before she could even flail her arms, she was tumbling backward. A strangled cry of surprise died in her throat when he gripped her arms and yanked her upright.

"Thank you," she said, holding on to his forearms to steady herself.

"You're welcome."

Still chuckling, he stepped back. A magazine slithered sideways, and suddenly they both were toppling toward a large box of discarded clothes and old winter sweaters.

"Aaa!" Georgie squealed, grabbing for Murdock and scrambling for a foothold on the slippery magazines.

With a presence of mind that Georgie found impressive, Murdock twisted his body, and instead of crashing to the floor like a felled tree, he sat with a hard jolt on top of the box, pulling Georgie down with him. Flung across a jean-clad lap, Georgie lifted her face from where it had squashed against his chest. Her eyes opened very wide. As she gazed into his gray eyes, she saw him grin broadly.

"We're saved," he said.

"Yes," Georgie replied, too stunned to move.

Then the box caved in. Under their combined weight, the cardboard sides collapsed, and they sank into a deep crater of fuzzy sweaters. Georgie gave a muffled cry and struggled to free herself from the jumbled sprawl of arms and legs.

"Ow!" Murdock growled from somewhere beneath her. "Don't put your knee there."

"Oh, good heavens!" Georgie moaned in mortification. "I'm so sorry."

Wriggling and twisting, she floundered helplessly on top of him. Her head was jammed under the arm of his leather jacket, her cheek pressed against his shirt. With one hand pinned beneath her side, the other draped over his chest and her legs sticking straight out of the box, she had somehow assumed a ridiculous parody of the backward-bowed swan dive.

"That's my face you've got your elbow in," he grunted. "And stop squirming like that."

"I'm trying to get out."

"I know that. But stop it, anyway."

Georgie tugged at her trapped arm. "What's wrong with you? Do you want to stay here all night?"

"If you keep wiggling like that, I do."

Reaching for the battered edge of the box, his words brought her up short. Surely she hadn't heard him right?

When her head snapped up, she caught the quick gleam of a slow, wolfish grin. Her heart skipped a beat. Oh, sweet Lord, Georgie thought in sudden realization. That wasn't his gun pressed against her stomach.

"Murdock—"

But he had pulled his hands free, and now he cupped her face in two large palms and drew her head down to his. His lips were full and warm, his kiss a velvet softness over hard insistence. At the first touch of his lips, Georgie's breath caught and held.

With slow deliberation he prolonged the kiss, holding her fast with his hands. Despite her astonishment, Georgie was vividly, almost painfully aware of every hard curve and muscled plane of his body. Pressed helplessly together in a tangle of limbs, she could feel his chest rise and fall with his quickened breathing, feel the muscle in his thigh jump and tighten as he shifted, feel the growing tautness in his body as he lingered long and purposefully on her lips.

His kiss was an invitation, a challenge . . . a forceful act of persuasion. And Georgie felt powerless to resist. With a soundless sigh, the surprised rigidness slowly ebbed from her body, and she relaxed against him, her soft flesh melting against the granite length of his body.

He must have sensed her surrender because his own body grew harder. With his mouth against hers, he inhaled deeply, almost savagely, as though to drink her in. His fingers left her face to tangle in her hair while, with one practiced hand, he skimmed the arch of her back.

She was never sure exactly how he managed it. One moment they were cramped together in the box, the next they had toppled over and spilled onto the floor. And never once had his lips left hers.

"Georgie," he murmured against her mouth.

She lay flat on the floor, and with one hand beside her head, he balanced himself over her, shrugging his leather jacket off first one shoulder, then the other. His strong thighs were between hers, pinning her. When he reached for the belt of her jeans, an instinctive, panicky alarm shrilled through her. Hurriedly, Georgie turned her face from his and grabbed for his hands.

"Murdock. Wait. Stop," she panted, breathless from his kisses.

He raised his head, his eyes closed. Hanging over her like that, with his chest heaving and his jaw clenched, he looked very male, very formidable and very much a stranger.

With a nervous swallow, Georgie pressed her palms against his chest, and nearly started at the heat of the smooth flesh under his shirt.

"Wait," she repeated, her heart hammering. "It's too fast. You're scaring me. I . . . I can't think."

At her words, he finally opened his eyes. Gray eyes, hot and blistering as molten steel, seared her with a long and searching gaze. His breath came in short, shallow rasps.

"Yes, you're right," he said at last, his voice low and strangled. "Slower."

"But I can't think what—"

"Don't think, Georgie," he said. His eyes held hers, intense and piercing. "There's nothing to be scared of and nothing to think about. Nothing but this."

When his mouth covered hers again, Georgie felt a brief flurry of protest that quickly weakened and died. What was there to think about? There was something. Something she knew she had to tell him. But his lips were so demanding, so full of urgent need, that her own body instinctively responded with a need of its own.

She wanted him, Georgie admitted. She wanted him as she'd never wanted anything in her life. And he was stirring up this desire, fanning it with his hands and his mouth into a fire she couldn't control. What was there to think about?

Nothing but this, Georgie sighed. When he pulled her shirt free of her jeans and slid a large, strong hand across the tender skin of her abdomen, she gave a moan of tortured pleasure.

Rising to his knees, he ripped his shirt over his head without bothering to unbutton it. His chest was thick and massive, sprinkled with fine, brown hairs and ridged with muscle. Georgie stared at him, an echo of her earlier apprehension rising in her.

He didn't give her a chance to succumb to the uncertainty a second time. With surprising gentleness, he hooked a strong arm around her waist, raising her toward him to slip first her jacket, then her shirt from her shoulders.

For a long moment he studied her as she leaned back against his arm in a lacy pink bra. His eyes closed, and Georgie saw the movement in his throat when he swallowed hard, as though he was struggling to control himself.

Slowly, he slipped the bra from her shoulders, his fingers lingering over the full, white roundness of her breasts and the pink, swollen nipples. Then he laid her softly down again, gave her an unexpectedly tender smile, smoothed a hand down her cheek and reached for his belt.

Sudden excruciating shyness overwhelmed her, and Georgie squeezed her eyes shut. Oh, why couldn't she be more sophisticated and nonchalant? she nearly wailed. If she was going to be seduced, couldn't she at least be a little more daring about it?

Forcibly, Georgie opened her eyes, just in time to see Murdock lower himself to the floor beside her. His eyes had darkened to a turbulent, stormy gray, but his smile was still gentle when he reached for the button on her jeans. Deliberately, Georgie willed herself to turn toward him, raising her hips when he slid her jeans and panties down her legs.

He was naked beside her, his skin smooth and golden and his body etched with the long lines of powerful muscles. Somehow, Georgie thought, he seemed a whole lot bigger without his clothes. Glancing down the flat plane of his stomach, Georgie's mouth went a little dry. Yes, she thought, much larger.

"Murdock, I—"

He stopped her words with a kiss. His fingers brushed her shoulders, leaving a tingling trail as they wandered across to the fluttering pulse at her neck, then down to the soft skin between her breasts.

"Come to me," he said quietly, his lips against hers. "Come to me, Georgie."

It was then that she knew he'd spoken the truth. There was nothing to be afraid of. Not from him. With sudden eagerness, Georgie raised her hands to his shoulders and pulled herself close to nestle against him.

The first shock of his bare skin on hers sent a shiver of dizzying longing through her, and she felt her heart skitter and race. Burying her face in the hollow between his neck and shoulder, she breathed in the raw, male scent of him.

Pulling back, he gazed down at her. Soft as a summer breeze, he skimmed his palm down the length of her body. The whispered touch of his hand sent shivers clear through to her soul, and she gave a muted gasp.

"My God," he breathed, finally meeting her eyes. "My God, you're even more beautiful than I'd imagined."

His hand brushed her belly, then cupped her breast, and he stroked her nipple with his thumb in such tormentingly gentle caresses, Georgie gave a tiny moan. Reaching up, she clutched the heavy muscles of his shoulders and tried to draw him down to her.

"Slowly," he said, and smiled. "Remember?"

She shook her head against the floor. "No. I don't."

He let her guide him, settling between her legs and raising himself on his forearms. Like drops of dew, he sprinkled tiny kisses on the hollows at her temples, on her cheeks, on her eyelids, and then he captured her lips with his once more.

The feel of his hard, solid body against hers was almost painfully sensual, and she moved under him restlessly, flushed with pleasure and aching for more. When he pushed her legs wider with a powerful thigh and lowered himself to her, she clung to his shoulders, returning his kisses with a fevered passion that matched his, moan for moan.

At the first thrust, Georgie nearly cried out. She clutched his shoulders and felt his muscles tighten and move under her hands. At the next plunge, she did cry aloud, but by then he was inside her, filling her with an ecstasy so sweet she could scarcely breathe.

They moved together in an ageless, ancient rhythm like the waxing and waning of the moon, the ebb and flow of the tides, the sunset and the sunrise. And then she was falling, tumbling headlong into the sweet black timelessness where there was only the salty wet taste of his skin on her tongue and the sound of his ragged breath in her ears.

7

MURDOCK LAY AWAKE in the dark room and watched Georgie sleep. He could see the pale outline of her soft cheek against his chest, the moon-shaped shadow of her lashes and the white of her fingers, curled in the hollow of his sternum. Her hair, lustrous and rich as chocolate, spread in a tangle over her shoulder and tickled his neck with its silkiness.

Good God, she was beautiful. As beautiful as the shimmer and dance of moonlight on dark water. If he were to reach out and grasp her to him, would she slip through his fingers as surely as the illusive, incandescent glimmer of a moonbeam? Would she, too, disappear?

Gently, hesitantly, he raised his hand and laid it on her arm. Her skin was creamy smooth and her flesh was firm and solid and real. Yet unaccountably, he felt no reassurance.

She lay beside him, nestled against his body with her breath warm against his skin. She was real, all right. But not for him. Tonight for one instant as he'd held her in his arms, their bodies twined together, he'd felt the earth shudder and quake beneath him. For that one moment the darkness had been ripped aside, and he'd seen a vision of something so peaceful and bright it had stolen his breath away.

Yet that had been an illusion, Murdock knew with bitter certainty—a misty glimpse of a far-off land he could never hope to reach. What she had to offer was not something he could take. Like the moonlight, he could never really capture and keep her in his hands.

Not him. Not now. It was too late for him. Too much had gone before. For too long he'd lived in darkness. He must have lost his mind tonight. It must have been a temporary fit of insanity that had made him reach for her, kiss her, drag her to him . . . make love to her. How could he have dared? Had he really thought he could walk into the light?

With a sleepy murmur Georgie moved beside him, snuggling closer against him. Before he could help himself, his arm tightened around her. The next moment, he forcibly relaxed his arm.

He'd lost control again, he told himself. That was what had happened. Somehow, she'd snuck by him when he wasn't looking. So beautiful and innocent, she'd made him laugh as he hadn't in years. Then when his guard was down, she'd slipped through the narrow chink and into his soul.

And yet it wasn't really as simple as that, was it? Because hadn't he wanted her to? Hadn't he hoped she would come? Hadn't he let her slip in? *He* was the one who'd made a grasp for the light, even as he'd known with complete certainty that it could never, ever be his.

In the breathless silence of the night, he could hear the soft inhalation of her breath, feel the warm, soft curve of her breast against his chest, and smell the faint perfume of her hair, caught in the whiskers on his chin. Long and sleek, her leg lay lightly over his, and he could see the tantalizing slope of her hip under the white sheet. A yawning hollow opened in the pit of Murdock's stomach, and he squeezed his eyes shut against the unexpected pain of it.

He was a fool, he told himself with sudden savagery. A damned fool. There was only one thing he could do, he knew. Slowly, with painstaking caution, he began to pull his arm from under her head.

Cool, slender fingers uncurled and splayed across his chest. A kiss as soft as a raindrop fell lightly on his bare skin, and he froze. With a rustle of sheets, she moved her leg and the velvety soft skin of her inner thigh brushed against him. Another feather-light kiss made his heart thud, and then she was raising herself and smiling sleepily at him.

Her green eyes were drowsy, misty with sleep, and her curved lips looked rosy and bruised.

"You're awake, too?" she asked in a whisper.

Unable to answer, he stared at her. How long had she been awake? he wondered. Could she have sensed, even in her sleep, the decision he'd made?

Her lids fluttered and a dark fringe of lashes lowered over the brilliant green of her gaze.

"Murdock," she began tremulously, and paused, looking into his eyes. "I need to tell you something."

At her words, so hesitant and ominous, a warning bell sounded somewhere deep in his consciousness. She was going to confide in him. She was going to confess something, and he didn't want to hear it. He had no right to know. Hadn't he just decided to leave her— leave her and never look back?

"Georgie, don't—"

"I'm pregnant," she said in a sudden breathless rush.

As though he'd been dropped from a very great height, Murdock lay in the center of the bed, stunned. Lights seemed to dance before his eyes. For one awful moment he'd thought she'd said—

"I'm sorry," she added in the same frightened flurry. "I should have told you. I would have. Honest, I would. But there wasn't—" She blushed deeply. "You didn't give me a chance."

"Pregnant?" he mouthed in utter astonishment. Slowly, the ridiculousness of her pronouncement filtered through to him. Turning on his side so that she slid off him and onto the bed, he looked at her flat belly under the sheet. Then he gazed long and hard at her.

"That's impossible," he said with authority. "We just had sex. You couldn't know."

Her own face went blank with surprise and her mouth dropped open. She gaped at him.

"What? Oh, no. Oh, Murdock. I didn't mean—" She gave him a quick, funny little smile. "I'm not *that* inexperienced."

He glowered at her in angry confusion. "Then what in God's name are you talking about?" he demanded.

"I'm pregnant. But it's not you." Her smile withered and died. "It was someone else."

Murdock's mouth went a little dry and his insides gave a single, sickening lurch. The world went black before his eyes. In a whirl of tormenting images he saw someone else touching her, someone else kissing her, some other man doing the things he'd done with her. And suddenly he thought he might go mad.

"Murdock?"

With a violent thrust, he flung aside the sheet and lunged from the bed. *You were leaving her,* his brain clamored at him. *You were leaving her, anyway.* It didn't matter, he told himself wildly. It didn't concern him.

"Murdock!"

At the door he turned back, his chest rising and falling heavily and his eyes clouded with unexplainable rage and despair. She was huddled against the headboard, clutching the sheet to her breasts and staring at him with anguished eyes.

My God, Murdock moaned silently, what had he done? She was pregnant. Another man. Dear God, what had he done?

"Please," she begged. "Please don't go like this. Let me explain—"

"There's nothing to explain," he growled. "Not to me."

"But there is. You're angry. Of course you are. I understand. But if you would just let me—"

Once more he stopped her. "I don't *want* to hear. All right? It's none of my business." Clenching his jaw and gripping the door so hard the edge cut into his palm, he continued in a slow, clear voice, "I'm sorry about last night. It should never have happened."

"You don't mean that. You can't mean—"

"It was my fault," he continued relentlessly. "And I take full responsibility. It won't ever happen again. I promise you that."

"Wait! Murdock!" she cried. Scrambling to her knees, she raised her hands to him, letting the sheet fall from her naked body. "Please, wait. Please, just listen to me."

Throwing open the door, he paused with his back to her and, before he could help himself, he said quietly, "You shouldn't have gotten into my car that first time. You should never have done it."

With a soft click that was somehow more final than the loudest slam, he shut the bedroom door and began to snatch his clothes from the living-room floor.

HOLDING A MANILA FOLDER absently, Georgie stared despondently into the filing cabinet and saw Murdock's face again, as it had been just before he'd shut the bedroom door behind him. Around her, the offices of Poulopoulos Investigations were bustling with the ringing of phones, the tinny clatter of the fax machine and the scurrying of half a dozen staff members dashing in and out. Yet this morning Georgie was aware of none of it.

She'd heard enough country and western songs in her life to be familiar with broken, bruised and bleeding hearts. She'd always thought they were a little silly in their exaggerations. Now she wasn't so sure. At this particular moment, it felt as if her insides had been torn out, and if that was an aching heart, then she had one.

Every time she thought of his words, of the way he'd hurled himself from the bed, then . . . then just walked away, she couldn't help flinching. Part of her wanted to burst into tears. The other part wanted to scream at the injustice and stupidity of it.

Okay, she thought now, gnawing the tip of her thumb. Okay, he'd been shocked that she was pregnant. What normal man wouldn't be? It's not exactly something men expect to hear from a woman they've just made love to. She could understand his dismay and confusion.

But to react like that! To tell her it was a mistake to have made love. To tell her he wished they'd never met. To practically shout that he never wanted anything more to do with her!

He'd made her feel ashamed and . . . and dirty. Closing her eyes, Georgie laid a hand against her stomach.

Maybe she *had* made a mistake. Maybe there was no "maybe" about it. But she wouldn't feel ashamed. She wouldn't feel guilty. Not when what was happening inside her was so wonderful and miraculous. She might wish that it had been someone other than Stuart. But no one—*no one*, Georgie repeated vehemently—would make her regret this baby.

Tears of sorrow and anger welled in Georgie's eyes, and viciously she rammed the folder into the row of files and slammed the drawer shut. The hell with Murdock, she thought with as much vehemence as she could muster. If he was going to be so callous and hard-hearted, well, she could match him with indifference. If he didn't care for her, well, then...she wouldn't care for him, either.

The childishness and utter hopelessness of that re-action left her drooping in despair. There was no way, Georgie admitted, that she could ever convince herself it didn't matter. Miserable and wretched, she turned from the filing cabinet.

Annie Dice stood several yards away, regarding her with puzzled concern.

"Is something wrong, Georgie?" she asked in her kind, even voice.

Taking a deep, steadying breath, Georgie shook her head.

"I'm only asking," Annie went on, "because you just filed the Belmont file in the N's."

Georgie gazed back at her, not quite trusting her voice to answer. To her horror, she felt a tear well up in the corner of her eye.

"I'm fine," she managed to utter as Annie gave her a compassionate look. "Really."

"Oh, my dear. I'm so sorry."

Georgie's look was startled.

"I know how much you want another case," Annie said. "And I know this isn't what you'd planned on— all this office work. But give your uncle time, Georgie. He's under a lot of pressure. Just be patient. Another case will come along, and he'll need extra help. You'll get a chance to prove yourself then. Believe me, he'll come 'round. You'll see."

"No," Georgie replied thoughtfully. "No, I don't think he will."

Only when she returned to her typewriter and the huge stack of reports that needed to be typed and filed did she realize that it wasn't really her uncle she'd been referring to.

OUTSIDE JIMMY RAY Thompson's apartment building, Murdock sat in his stuffy car, littered with paper coffee cups and empty takeout bags, and muttered crossly to himself. The entire case was going to hell, he silently fumed. His one solid lead in the whole damned mess was Jimmy Ray, and God only knew where *he'd* been all night.

Naturally, Reilly hadn't been anywhere to be found at four o'clock that morning when Murdock arrived. And when Jimmy Ray had suddenly shown up out of nowhere at noon, blithely whistling as he unlocked the front door and let himself into the building, Murdock had beat the steering wheel in frustration. Where the hell had the skinny little weasel been all night?

Scowling blackly at the apartment now, Murdock snatched a disposable cup from the dash, glanced at the cold dregs of coffee in the bottom and hurled the cup into the back seat with a curse. The overcooked hamburgers he'd eaten earlier for lunch sat heavy in his gut, his muscles ached from sitting so long in one position and his eyes burned with weariness.

He'd never been a particularly good-natured man even at the best of times, Murdock acknowledged, but today his mood went beyond being merely foul. He felt like beating someone to a pulp—like wrenching the steering wheel out of the dash, like kicking at the car door until it buckled and crumpled, like bellowing in fury until he went hoarse. He felt like leaning his head back against the seat, raising his fists to his eyes . . . and wailing. Wailing like some stupid kid.

Breathing heavily, Murdock gripped the steering wheel with shaking hands and lowered his forehead. The case was getting to him. That was all. This damned case seemed to go everywhere and nowhere at once, and half the time he wasn't even sure what he was still doing on it. Maybe he was just overtired. Maybe he'd pushed himself too hard, and now he was paying the consequences.

Murdock sat up, staring out the windshield at Jimmy Ray's apartment without really seeing it. Certainly it wasn't because of *her*. No, that was laughable. Men with jobs like his didn't get entangled with women. They weren't any good at it. And anyway, they couldn't afford the distraction . . . not if they valued their lives.

No, Murdock told himself, he wasn't bothered by Georgie. She was just a woman. He'd had plenty of women in his time, and he'd walked cleanly away from every one of them without a single regret. Since that horrible night six years ago, he'd made very sure that he never let another person get too close, and he wasn't about to change that decision anytime soon.

Sure, there were appealing things about her, but nothing he couldn't get from any other woman. Briefly,

Murdock remembered with almost painful vividness the way she'd felt under him, clinging to him and murmuring tiny, gasping moans of pleasure as her body moved fluidly with his. He gripped the steering wheel more tightly.

No, it wasn't Georgie that made him want to put his fist through the windshield. He didn't care about her. She was nothing to him. Yeah, maybe he had skated a little too close to the edge this time. He'd hung around too long. He'd let his guard down and almost started wondering what it might be like to stay.

But he hadn't stayed. Thank God, he'd come to his senses. He'd gotten out in time.

Across the street, a middle-aged woman walked up the sidewalk to the apartment building, balancing two shopping bags on her hips and hauling a small, fluffy dog behind her on a leash. Murdock watched her fumble in her bag for her keys, unlock the door and disappear inside. He sighed, and began to search among the jumble of papers and trash for his thermos.

From the corner of his eye, he saw a car streak by. The next instant, he sat upright in the seat and gaped out the window with incredulous eyes. A small red Volkswagen jerked to a stop alongside the curb half a block away.

Murdock stared at the car as his face slowly stiffened with annoyance. He waited, his hands clenching the forgotten thermos. But when no one appeared from the car, he knew. Of course, he'd known. Georgie had come by after work. She was going to stay on the case.

Murdock tossed the thermos heedlessly on the seat beside him. The frustration and anger that had rankled and chafed him all day suddenly rose in him. Impulsively, he threw open his door, without giving himself a chance to consider what he might say. Propelled forward by a wave of ill-temper, he slammed his door, yanked at his hat and stalked down the street past the line of parked cars.

The evening sky was a dark, stormy purple, and a brisk wind had begun to gather in gusts on the street corners, stirring leaves and bits of newspaper in the gutters. There was a smell of dampness in the air, and even as Murdock reached the Volkswagen and halted beside the driver's-side window, a thin splinter of lightning streaked across the darkening sky.

His sharp rap made her jump. Her face was a blur of white, staring out at him. A moment later, she rolled down the window.

She'd pulled her glossy brown hair back in a single thick braid again, though wispy strands had escaped and curled loosely around her face. The white shirt she wore under a richly embroidered vest was voluminous, made for a man twice her size. She looked lost in it.

For a long moment, they gazed wordlessly at each other. Perhaps it was a trick of the growing dusk, but he thought her eyes looked dark and shadowed, like the deep green water in a pool shaded from the sun. The silent look she gave him was wary.

Murdock balled his fists and gestured at her car with a quick jerk of his head.

"What're you doing here?" he demanded curtly.

She stared back at him, not speaking.

"Haven't you had enough yet?" he continued. "Or do you still think playing detective is all fun and games?"

Her eyes narrowed. "This is my case," she said, her voice low and emotionless. "I'm going to solve it."

"Oh, really? And how do you propose to do that? By getting yourself killed like Walters and Howard Kavin?"

She shot him a tight, angry look and started to roll up her window. Quick as a flash, he stepped forward and curled his fingers around the edge. Bending low, he brought his face close to hers.

"It's over, Georgie," he said firmly. "You and I have run the gamut. The whole way. There's nothing more to come. Do you understand? I'm not going to help you anymore."

"Fine." She bit off the word. "Then don't. I don't need your help. I can solve this case on my own."

"On your own?" He glowered at her. A drop of rain struck one of his hands still wrapped around the edge of the window. "You've got to be kidding. You don't know what you're doing, and you have no idea what you're up against. Keep it up and the only thing you'll get is a slab in the morgue."

Her eyes flickered uneasily, but she raised her small chin. "I know what I'm doing, and I know as much about the case as you do. If my being here makes *you* uncomfortable, then maybe *you* should find something else to work on."

"What the hell is that supposed to mean?"

"You know perfectly well what I mean. I'm talking about last night."

"Last night has nothing—"

She shifted on the seat to look down at her hands, clasped in her lap. "You changed your mind this morning. All right. I can accept that."

"I don't see what that has to do with—"

She raised her head, and he thought he saw her mouth tremble. "I think you're selfish and insensitive, but that doesn't matter. Do whatever you want. But don't try to stop me from doing my job just because you feel guilty."

"Guilty? I don't feel guilty. Why should I?" Murdock stepped back a pace, releasing the window. A dull heaviness spread in his gut, and he had to look away from her to say the next words. "For God's sake, grow up, Georgie. Things happen. Last night got a little out of control. That's all. I already apologized this morning."

Fat, lazy drops splattered on the street. Several splashed on the toes of his boots. When he looked back at her, her face was stricken. He could have sworn her cheeks paled. The heavy weight in his stomach pressed down on him.

"I see," she said slowly. "Last night was just a silly little mistake."

Something mocking in her voice made him frown in discomfort. "Well, yes. If you want to put it that way."

With a small, stifled sound, she leaned forward and began to work furiously to roll up the window. Startled, Murdock leaped toward the rapidly disappearing crack and nearly got his fingers crushed as the window snapped shut.

"Damn it!"

For a split second their eyes met through the glass. Then he sprang for the door handle just as she reached over her shoulder to slam home the lock. His pull was so forceful he nearly yanked the door off its hinges.

Momentarily, she stared at him through the open door, then swiveled in the seat to turn her back on him. Uncertainly he stood there, breathing hard, while the rain fell more steadily around him. He was nuts, Murdock told himself. Why didn't he just go back to his car and forget about her?

"Look," he said gruffly, doing his best to suppress his rising exasperation. "Don't be such a damned little idiot. This isn't a game, Georgie. This case is serious, and I'm not going to be around anymore to watch out for you. Can't you get that into your head? It's too dangerous for you to be playing detective in, er, in your condition."

Very slowly she turned to him, her eyes widening. She gave him an infuriated glare and said tightly, "In my, my—"

He cut her off crisply. "Are you willing to risk this kind of danger when you're carrying a child?"

Overhead a loud thunderclap rent the air, and Murdock stared down at Georgie, suddenly arrested. Despite himself, a cold horror stole into his heart and, with it, a shattering sense of déjà vu.

"Unless," he added quietly, "you aren't going to have it."

Almost inarticulate with indignation, she sputtered, "What! How dare— Of course I'm going to have it. Not that it's any of your business. Now, let go of my door!"

"What about the child then? Have you thought of your child?"

In that moment, he realized that she was well and truly livid. Her eyes flashed green sparks of fury, her creamy complexion was flushed with a rosy heat and her voice trembled with emotion. Despite himself, he felt a warm glow of admiration and more than a little desire.

"You, you—you obnoxious jerk!" she stammered. "How dare you tell me what to think? *You*, of all people! What do you care? The second you learned I was pregnant, you bolted out the door as fast as your legs could carry you. Well, you can just bolt away again. I don't need you. I can handle this case on my own. In fact, I've got some very important information which will probably solve the whole thing."

Surprised, Murdock loosened his hold on the door. "What information? What are you talking about?"

"That's my business. Now leave me alone. I've had enough of you."

With a suddenness that took him off guard, she pounced at the door. Giving it a tremendous tug, she tore it from his grasp, slammed it shut and locked it before he'd scarcely drawn a breath.

Murdock stood beside the car, his hands at his sides and the rain dripping off the brim of his hat and trickling down the back of his neck. She'd called him an obnoxious jerk, which was probably true. He wasn't going to argue the point. But that still didn't change the fact that she was being a belligerent little fool.

"Georgie?" Murdock shouted at the window. "What information? Georgie? Open this door!"

From inside the car, her voice sounded raw with anger. "No! Go away."

"Georgie—"

"Go *away*, I said."

"Georgie . . . Damn it!"

"I don't want to talk to you. I never want to talk to you again. Not for as long as I live."

Rain streamed down the window, and her shape was indistinct in the growing darkness.

"That might not be as long as you'd like," Murdock shouted again, bending toward the car. "You realize that, don't you? Whatever your information is, forget about it. Forget about the case and go home, or you might not make it through next week."

Only silence answered him.

"Did you hear me, Georgie? I said you should go home. The street is no place for a woman in your condition. You don't belong out here with the—"

A sudden deafening blare drowned out his words. From inside the car came the loud wail of a rock song. She'd turned on the radio full blast.

With the toe of his shoe, Murdock kicked the front tire of the Volkswagen. He glared at the car. Jamming his hands into the pockets of his overcoat, he grumbled a long string of curses at the rain, the night, Jimmy Ray Thompson, his client, and the Volkswagen, particularly the young woman inside it.

Stymied and bristling at the unusual taste of defeat, Murdock scraped his boots against the pavement, shot a last glower at the car and slowly made his way back to the Buick.

GEORGIE SAT inside her car, silently fuming, occasionally sniffling and absently shredding a tissue into tiny pieces with her fingers. Rain drummed on the roof, breaking the silence.

Since she'd flicked off the radio, which she'd only turned on to hide the short but violent storm of tears that had suddenly overcome her, the rain was the only thing to listen to. An early spring thunderstorm, it seemed to pour from the sky, running in sheets down the steamed windows and beating a rumbling tattoo on the car.

With a loud hiccup, a remnant from her crying jag, Georgie turned to the window. She wiped a clear spot on the foggy glass and peered out. The apartment building was all but invisible in the downpour.

Jimmy Ray wasn't going to venture out in this weather, Georgie knew. It was ridiculous to sit here waiting for him, especially as she needed a rest room worse than anything and was practically starving to death for a double cheeseburger with extra pickles. What in the world was she doing out here in the rain?

Leaning back with a sigh, she closed her eyes and wondered if *he* was still somewhere out there in the rain. He was probably sitting in his car, stewing over the lie she'd told about having important information. Most likely, his only concern was how to get it out of her.

Oh, why did it have to hurt so much? If only she didn't care what Murdock thought.

But, Georgie admitted, she did care. She cared desperately. His criticism of her abilities as a detective smarted like a slap. His description of their night together as an insignificant mistake stung and throbbed like a blistering burn. But it was his obvious lack of feeling for her that hurt worst of all.

He didn't care for her, Georgie told herself. She was nothing but a headache to him—an unwelcome nuisance. Certainly he didn't love her, and that knowledge cut through her like a razor-sharp knife.

Even as the thought formed in her mind, Georgie stiffened and went still. Love? Good heavens, what was she doing thinking about love? Surely she'd learned enough to know that love, even at its best, was a perilous gamble. Love with Murdock would be downright deadly—as swift and certain as sticking her head in an oven.

She wasn't in love with Murdock, Georgie reassured herself with a small, apprehensive smile. Of course she wasn't! How ridiculous to think that—

That everything he thought or felt about her mattered? That she longed for him to take her in his arms again and kiss away her fears? That she missed talking to him, seeing him, laughing with him, just being in the same place with him?

Stunned, Georgie fell back in her seat, her heart thudding in panic. Oh, no! she nearly cried aloud. She couldn't have fallen in love with Murdock. She *couldn't* have. She knew better than that. It simply couldn't be.

Yet even as she denied it, Georgie knew she'd stumbled onto the truth.

WITH A SHAKE of his head, Murdock flicked the rain from his face, ran a hand over his wet hair and squinted into the darkness. Jimmy Ray, he'd decided, wasn't going to risk his fancy alligator boots in this storm. Although even if the guy did appear, Murdock admitted, he wasn't sure he would follow him tonight.

What the devil did she know that he didn't? Murdock asked himself again.

A peal of thunder broke overhead, echoing through the night. Murdock shook the rain from his face again. He'd discovered that, by craning his neck from the open window, he could just make out the left taillight of the red Volkswagen, and at the moment it seemed more judicious to keep his eye on Georgie than on Jimmy Ray.

Good Lord, he thought. What if she really *had* found something out? She wasn't going to tell him what it was. That much was clear.

But what if she went off on her own? If she somehow managed to ditch him and went after this lead by herself, she could be walking into all sorts of danger. How would she defend herself? With growing horror, Murdock considered all the ways of getting rid of a small, helpless female who happened to be a little too nosy.

And it wasn't just guns or well-placed blows to the head that had him almost frantic with worry. What if someone pushed her and she fell? Hell, one good scare might be all it took. He'd heard that women could lose babies after the least little fright.

Swallowing anxiously, Murdock wiped the rain from his eyes and stared hard at the taillight. It was useless to tell himself not to care—that it wasn't any of his business. He'd been telling himself that for the last two hours, and it hadn't done any good. His heart still went cold at the image of her wandering innocently into a meeting with some unscrupulous felon. His hands still shook at the thought of her stumbling onto the Meckelmann jewels . . . still attached to Walters and Kavin's killer.

He didn't want anything more to do with her, he reminded himself. Yet he wasn't about to live with her blood on his hands, either. If she was going to be stupid enough to strike out on her own, then he had little choice but to tail her.

As though his last thought had some mysterious, telepathic effect, the taillights of the Volkswagen suddenly came to life, gleaming an eerie red in the rain. Muttering under his breath, Murdock turned the key in the ignition, reversed the car, then inched the Buick into the street.

He waited for her to turn the corner. Then, with a passing glance at Jimmy Ray's lighted windows, Murdock started after Georgie.

On Fairmont Avenue, he began to breathe a little easier. It looked as though she might just be going home, after all. Yet when she sped by without turning onto her own street, his heart sank.

She was probably only stopping at the supermarket, he reassured himself. Or maybe she had to pick up her dry cleaning. The fact that they'd already passed three markets and half a dozen cleaners somewhat dampened his enthusiasm for that explanation, but still he held on to his hope until they'd traveled nearly ten miles north.

By the time the Volkswagen began to wind through a hilly section of older neighborhoods, Murdock's apprehension had grown by leaps and bounds. These neighborhoods were awfully damned close to the area Howard Kavin had told Georgie he was from, Murdock remembered. Could she have found out something about Kavin?

As vigilant and alert as he was, when Murdock climbed a long hill and finally reached the top, Georgie's car was nowhere in sight. Cold fear bit at his gut as he slowed the Buick, scanning the houses around him with sharp, experienced eyes.

Despite the dread that fluttered in his chest—or perhaps because of it—he slipped easily and almost automatically into a state of emotionless, calculating efficiency, an ability that had once made him such a valuable commodity to the military. The role of relentless professional hunter had been one he was well-suited for and it had been so carefully drilled into him that even now it practically felt like a second skin.

With his foot lightly tapping the brake, Murdock coasted slowly down the hill, taking in every house and driveway, every car and movement. Halfway down he was rewarded with a glimpse of red. Down a short side street, nearly a block away, the car was partially hidden from view behind a large bush. Turning the wheel sharply, Murdock parked the Buick under the overhanging branches of a tree and contemplated the rear fender of the red Volkswagen.

Under the shelter of the leafy awning, he could watch the heavy, gusting curtains of rain sweeping down the street and across well-tended lawns. The houses were redbrick, old but conscientiously maintained. It didn't look like the sort of place where someone could run into trouble, and that—above all—made him suspicious.

Opening the glove compartment, he pulled out a 9mm Beretta, checked the magazine, slammed it home with the heel of his hand and slipped the gun into the empty holster under his arm. He'd long ago disconnected or taped over all the interior lights in the car, but when he opened the door, he did it cautiously nonetheless.

Under the dripping boughs of the trees, he stooped low and began to move forward in a quick, crouching run, skirting the dim circle of lights from decorative lampposts and clinging to the protective cover of hedges and vine-covered fences. When he reached the red car, he squatted behind the back fender, pulled the gun from his holster and slowly peered over the vehicle to the brick house at the end of the driveway.

Lights burned in the front windows, and as he watched, an indistinct shadow flitted in front of one of the windows, then disappeared. Soundlessly, Murdock followed the line of bushes and trees to the back of the house. With a deep breath, he hurled himself across the gravel driveway, over an open stretch of lawn and into the shadowy darkness by the back door.

For a long time, he stood outside the door with his back to the wall and the 9mm held between his two hands. Every nerve in his body was strained and taut as he listened to the wail of the wind, the splattering of rain off the roof and the faint, almost imperceptible murmur of distant voices from inside the house.

For one indecisive moment, he hesitated, wavering. And then he heard it. In the midst of the low hum of voices, he heard the sound of a woman crying. It was a low, nearly inaudible series of sobs, but its effect on Murdock was instantaneous and lethal.

With a savage growl of barbaric ferocity, he kicked in the back door, bounded across a brightly lit kitchen and poised himself in firing stance in the doorway to a dining room. The group around the large wooden table turned white, frightened faces toward him, and he nearly smiled at their fear.

"Let her go," he said between his teeth. "Georgie. Come on."

Across the room, Georgie staggered to her feet, her face as pale as the others who circled the table. With a swell of murderous rage, he noticed her face was streaked with tears.

"Murdock!" she gasped. "What in the world are you doing? Have you lost your mind?"

"We'll talk about this later," he growled. "Just get over here."

"Good grief!" she cried, throwing up her arms in a gesture of frustration. "I can't believe you followed me. You *tailed* me. How could you? And for Pete's sake, don't point that gun at my mother!"

8

As THOUGH Georgie's words tripped an invisible switch, the entire Poulopoulos family was instantly galvanized into action. The dining room became a scene of uncontrolled bedlam, filled with a flurry of screams and half swoons, scraping chair legs and smashing crockery, wails of fright and thunderous male voices demanding explanations.

"Oh, sweet Lord," Georgie breathed, rolling her eyes toward the ceiling. She dropped heavily back into her chair.

From the kitchen doorway, Murdock's gaze was glued to hers, his cool gray eyes slowly registering understanding . . . and dawning horror. If she hadn't felt so wretched and guilty, she probably would have giggled. He *did* look awfully ridiculous, looming there in that forbidding stance with his legs straddled wide, his hat sopping wet and misshapened, and his coat dripping on her mother's polished floor.

Weakly, Georgie waved a hand in his direction. "Put the gun away, Murdock," she said wearily. "Before you shoot my family."

"Your family?" he asked in a hollow, stricken voice.

"He has a gun! Cosmo, he has a gun!" Georgie's mother screeched.

"What the hell?" her oldest brother, Alexi, bellowed as her brother Demetri jumped to his feet, knocking over his chair.

"We're going to be killed," her sister Mary shrieked, and grabbed Georgie's other sister around the shoulders. "We're going to die, Theresa!"

Theresa brushed her off and clung in terror to her new husband.

"Look, buddy," Stefan said, his hands raised as he took a step forward, "why don't you give me that gun? Hmm? Just give me the gun, and we can talk—"

"Let's get him, Alexi!" Demetri hollered, and lowered his head as though to rush the doorway.

"Hold on, *everyone!*"

Like a furious bull, Cosmo rose to his feet at the head of the table, his massive shoulders hunched and his face dark with anger. The sound of his mallet-sized fists striking the table still reverberated in the air as he surveyed the room, fixing each member of his hysterical family with a threatening stare.

In the ensuing silence, little Anthony approached Murdock, his head tilted curiously to look up at the gun and into the face of the damp intruder.

"My sister Georgie's going to have a baby," he told Murdock proudly.

Georgie's mother wailed aloud.

"Oh, good grief," Georgie moaned, and sank farther down in her seat.

Murdock's gaze was still riveted on her, his eyes glazed with shock. He gave a bewildered shake of his head, showering the doorway with drops of water. Then very slowly he lowered the gun and looked down at Georgie's little brother. Befuddled, he stared at Anthony.

"Yes," Murdock said in a dazed voice. "I know she is."

Georgie covered her eyes with her hands and groaned.

"What the hell?" Alexi repeated.

"You *know* this person?" Demetri demanded of Georgie.

Georgie heard her mother murmur, "Oh, sweet mother of God," before she laid her head on the table.

"Uh-oh," Mary said, and giggled.

"Georgie?" Stefan whirled to stare at her, appalled.

With a loud crash, Cosmo's chair fell backward. *"Him?"* he thundered. Raising a meaty hand, he pointed across the table at Murdock. *"You?"*

In the act of holstering his gun, Murdock paused. His head snapped up, and Georgie met his gaze in a silent, horrified appeal. She saw his eyes flicker with sudden, staggering understanding, then his face went completely, perfectly blank.

"You?" Cosmo repeated, his nostrils flaring and his breath coming in sharp, furious blasts.

Numb with shock, Georgie still somehow managed to spring to her feet. "Dad, no!"

But it was too late. Her three older brothers and her father had already begun to advance, her newest brother-in-law hanging behind in a halfhearted show of solidarity.

Georgie had always thought of her father and brothers as large men, the kind other men usually backed down from pretty quickly. Yet, as they circled Murdock, he towered over them, broad-shouldered and brawny, like a redwood among saplings. Still, there was only one of him. Despite his powerful size, the Poulopoulos men had him outnumbered, and they were fast closing ranks.

Frantic now, Georgie scrambled over chairs and around the table in a desperate attempt to put an end to this madness. Running up against a wall of broad, masculine backs, she tugged furiously on the two nearest shirts.

"Wait! Stop! Dad! Dad, listen to me. It's not him. He's not the one. It *isn't* him."

Over his shoulder, Alexi scowled at her. "Go sit down, Georgie. We'll handle this."

Georgie yanked at her father's arm. "Dad, please. Listen to me. He's not the father. Please, Dad."

Cosmo shook off her hand. "Don't try to protect him, Georgie." He glared at Murdock. "Let him stand up for himself. Be a man."

With a cry of dismay, Georgie tried to squeeze between her brothers.

Cosmo eyed Murdock blackly. "So, you. Just what do you propose to do about my daughter?"

"Murdock, run!" Georgie squealed as she wiggled and squirmed in a vain attempt to slip between two solid bodies.

Standing stiff and tense in the center of an ominous ring of Poulopoulos men, Murdock stared back at them with a wooden expression. Reaching up, he pulled off his hat.

"Well?" Cosmo demanded with a growl.

"Oh, please! Won't any of you listen to me?" Georgie wailed.

"Sir," Murdock unexpectedly snapped. "I haven't given it much thought, sir."

Cosmo gaped at him, then hardened his jaw. "Well, you'd damned well better give it some thought pretty damned quick, hadn't you?"

"Yes, sir," Murdock answered briskly.

"Oh, for God's sake," Georgie cried, and kicked Demetri in the leg. "Stop this! Let me through!"

"What was all this business with the gun?" Alexi barked.

Georgie thought she heard Murdock clear his throat. "That was a misunderstanding."

"A *misunderstanding?*" Cosmo bellowed. "I'll say it was a misunderstanding. You damned scoundrel, I ought to wring your neck!"

"Dad, no!"

"Sir," Murdock said evenly.

"And what about Georgie?" Cosmo repeated. "I want to know what you're going to do about my daughter. If you think you can shirk your responsibility to her, you've got another think coming."

"For heaven's sake, Murdock," Georgie shouted. "Just tell them the truth."

"No, sir," Murdock said gravely. "I never shirk my responsibilities."

"Murdock!" Georgie howled.

"Let's take him outside, Dad," Demetri said hotheadedly. "This creep took advantage of Georgie. Let's beat the hell out of him."

"Oh, shut up, Demetri," Stefan muttered, and took a step back.

With a stifled cry of alarm, Georgie pounced at the opening he left. Large, drenched and completely composed, Murdock stood in the doorway. His gaze met hers, and for an instant she almost thought she spied a glimmer of sardonic humor in his cool gray eyes.

"Did I hear you say you're going to do right by my daughter?" Cosmo asked Murdock, some of the anger already leaving his voice.

"Sir," Murdock answered, releasing Georgie's gaze and turning to her father. "I think that Georgie might have something to say about it." Almost under his breath, he added, "She usually does."

Cosmo peered down at her. "Georgie?"

For a panicked moment, Georgie thought she might just fall to the floor in a dead faint. Stupefied and confused, she gaped at Murdock, then at her father, then at the whole group of men.

"She's too upset to speak," Cosmo pronounced, turning back to Murdock.

"Yes, sir. I suppose she is," Murdock agreed. "We haven't really had a chance to talk about things. Have we, Georgie?"

Georgie thought she heard a wicked, teasing note in his voice. Although no one else seemed to hear it. She wondered, in a flood of disorienting astonishment, if he was laughing at her. Opening her mouth, she tried to speak, but no sound came out.

"I guess we'd better go and talk things over," Murdock went on. The hint of laughter in his voice was unmistakable now...as was the dangerous glint in his eyes. "If you don't mind, sir, I think we'll go now. Georgie?"

"Huh?" She gaped at him, slack-jawed.

"Ready?"

She blinked. "What?"

"Let's go."

Georgie stirred herself. "Eh? Oh. Oh, yes. Okay. I'm coming."

"Now."

"Right." She snatched her coat from the back of a chair, gave her assembled family a wild-eyed stare and felt Murdock's hand close over her arm.

Lifting his hat, he nodded curtly once, said "Good night, folks," and jammed the hat back on his head. Before she could call goodbye or even raise her arm to wave, he'd dragged her through the door and across the kitchen.

The last thing she heard before the back door slammed behind them was her father's voice rumbling in a loud, forced attempt at cheerfulness, "Well, at least he knows how to handle her. That's something, I guess."

"JUST WHAT in heaven's name do you think you're doing? Are you crazy? Have you completely lost your mind? Murdock? What in the world were you thinking? Do you realize what a mess you've created? Do you? Oh, this is horrible. Just awful. I can't believe you..."

Ignoring her breathless jabbering, Murdock hauled Georgie down the driveway through the rain and didn't pause until they'd reached her car. There, he suddenly turned, folded his arms across his chest and gave her such a look that her indignant tirade died off.

"And just what was I supposed to do?" he finally asked. "Proclaim my innocence?"

"Yes," she snapped, irritably shaking rain out of her eyes. "That might not have been a bad idea."

"Except that no one would have believed me. Did you see your brother? The stocky one with the mole—"

"Demetri."

"—wanted to tear my head off. If I'd denied a single word, he would have tried to put his fist down my throat."

Unable to dispute the truth in that, she gave him a baffled, stymied look, then drew her eyebrows together angrily. Throwing up her arms in despair, she shouted, "But don't you see what you've done? Now they all think that . . . They all believe that . . ."

"That I'm the father of your child," Murdock finished for her. With a shock, he realized the phrase generated a warm, pleasant glow in the pit of his stomach. Quickly, he suppressed it.

"Yes," she said sharply. "Exactly."

"I didn't actually have much choice in the matter," he defended.

"Choice? You had every choice in the book. For starters, you could have stayed away. You shouldn't have even *been* here."

Murdock frowned at that. "I have to admit that was a mistake on my—"

"What were you doing here in the first place? You followed me here, didn't you?"

Murdock stared at the ground, wondering if it would do any good to lie, and decided the situation was pretty hopeless. He was going to have to bluster his way through. He scowled at her from beneath the brim of his hat.

"Yeah? So? Sure, I followed you. I thought you might get into trouble, so I—"

"In trouble?" she fumed. "Oh, I'm in trouble, all right. I'm in so much trouble right now, I don't know where to begin. Thanks to you. To be completely honest, half of my problems now are all *your* fault."

With a haughty toss of her head, she reached for the Volkswagen's door handle, slipping a little in the wet, slick gravel.

"Well, I think you *should* thank me," Murdock floundered, his own temper rising as she turned her back on him. "Because obviously you haven't told them who the real father is."

When she spun back around, her face was pinched and draining quickly of color. Seeing that look, he took a gamble and asked, "In fact, you weren't planning on ever telling them, were you?"

"That's none of your business," she replied curtly, but her eyes were anxious.

A hard lump of something bitter and noxious like bile formed in his craw. Helplessly, unable to stop himself, he pressed her harder. "Because he was the jerk you told me about? The one who was so famous? Oh, yeah, Georgie. I remember, all right. What's so special about this guy that you feel you have to protect him?"

Her eyes flickered to the house, then back to his face. "It has nothing to do with . . . He's not . . ."

She swallowed hard and gave him such an urgent, pleading look that Murdock felt his gut twist.

He held his fists at his sides. "You still care about this guy, is that it?"

"No!" Her cry was quick and utterly convincing. "No, that's not it. I just . . ." Her voice trailed off. Then suddenly, she raised her chin and said defiantly, "I'm ashamed, all right? There, now you know. I'm ashamed that it ever happened. It was just one night, and it was horrible. Worst of all, he never told me he was married."

With a sharp movement of his head, Murdock briefly closed his eyes as though he'd been slapped. The raw burning in his chest slowly dissipated and was replaced by something even more painful—regret.

"Georgie," he said. "I'm sorry. I'm sorry I—"

"Well, forget it," she said shortly. "It doesn't matter. The only thing that's important is this baby, and *that* is not something I'm sorry about."

An unexpected swell of admiration made him smile. "Well," he said more lightly, "at least your family's off your back now."

She gave him an uneasy look.

Taking a backward step, he threw his arms open to the rain and gave a stiff, little bow. "They have their scapegoat."

Her eyes widened. "What! You?"

"Why not? They already think I'm the father. Why not just let them go on thinking it? It can't hurt anyone."

"Because," she said intently, "you don't know my family. They aren't going to stop meddling now."

"Let them meddle. I know how to make myself scarce."

"I have a lot of brothers," she said with some urgency. "Quite a few uncles and cousins, too."

"I can take care of myself."

She stared at him, her face puzzled and thoughtful. With her head tilted to the side like that and her hair lying damp and tangled around her face, she looked incredibly young and innocent . . . and almost irresistibly sexy.

"But why?" she asked softly. "I thought you didn't want anything more to do with me. Why would you do that for me?"

For a brief, shuttered moment, Murdock thought of the child she carried, then of another child from the past, a child he had never known.

With careful deliberation, he answered, "Maybe I'm not doing it for you."

He saw her quick movement, the hand she nearly placed against her stomach, then hastily drew back. With a hard, crusty smile, he shook his head. "No," he said quietly. "Not that, either."

"But I don't under—"

"Maybe," he began with an unsteady breath, "maybe it's for me."

Her sharp look was surprised and questioning.

In a long, deep sigh, he let out his breath. "No, I'm not going to tell you about it. Maybe someday. But not now. Not tonight. So don't even bother to ask."

A funny little half smile began to grow on her lips. "Someday? But I thought we were finished. I thought you'd washed your hands of me. We'd run the gamut, remember?"

He eyed her with mock reproach, his eyes narrowed but twinkling. His short burst of laughter was full of irony without bitterness.

"Yeah, yeah. I remember. But a man's got to play the cards as they fall." Reaching around her, he pulled open the door of the Volkswagen. "Come on. Get in. We've got places to go and people to see."

Her smile wavered. "We do?"

"Yeah, we do. You want to meet Greenwood, don't you?"

She stiffened, then suddenly her face shone. "No kidding?"

"No kidding."

"But—"

"Let's just say that taking you with me is my one sure way of keeping you from going off and getting yourself killed."

About to duck into the car, she paused and glanced uneasily at him. "Murdock, I think there's something you should know. If you're only doing this to find out that information I said I had, you might be a little disappointed. The truth is that—"

"You don't know squat," he interrupted. "Yeah, I already figured that one out."

"You know? But... You aren't mad that I lied to you?"

"Sure I'm mad. Don't forget your seat belt."

Setting off down the driveway toward his own car, Murdock tugged off his hat and rubbed a hand over his wet hair. *Whoa, buddy,* a small voice whispered inside his head. *Big mistake. That was a very, very big mistake.*

"So what the hell am I supposed to do? Sit back and watch her wander blindly into danger?" he muttered to himself, slapping his hat on his leg as he walked.

It's not really as simple as that, is it?

"Don't be an idiot," Murdock mumbled. "She's a nice kid. That's all. I just don't want to see her end up like Walters."

At the sound of the Volkswagen backing up, he stepped to the edge of the driveway. Georgie pulled up beside him and gave him a strange, perplexed look. Squinting into the rain, she peered over his shoulder into the darkness.

"Is there someone else out here with us?" she asked, her voice a little worried.

"Eh? Uh, no. Uh, I was... I was just..." Frowning deeply, he looked at his hat, then suddenly crammed it back on his head.

"Hell," he said once more, and disappeared into the dripping trees.

IN THE BAR of the Landis Hotel, Murdock weaved through clusters of small cocktail tables toward the back, with Georgie following behind. They'd gone by her apartment to drop off her car, and she'd taken the opportunity to change into dry clothes and lend Murdock a shirt she'd swiped from one of her brothers. She'd also made him hand over his hat and brought it somewhat back to life with a blow-dryer.

As they stopped before a tall, thin man with a mustache, sitting alone, Georgie saw Murdock tug at the sleeves of the shirt which was several sizes too small for him.

"Greenwood," Murdock acknowledged.

The man stood up and regarded Georgie with distrustful eyes.

"I don't think you've met my—" Murdock gave her a quick, barely noticeable wink "—assistant. Georgie Polo—er, Polopi— "

"Pouloupoulos," Georgie said brightly, and held out her hand.

After a second's hesitation, Greenwood took it reluctantly in his own, gave her fingers a limp squeeze and dropped his hand.

"You didn't tell me anyone else knew about this case," Greenwood said in a reedy, complaining voice. "I think you should have told me there was someone else working with you."

"Well, I'm telling you now, aren't I?" Murdock said easily.

Pulling out a chair, he sat down, settled a booted foot on the knee of his other leg and crossed his arms. Nonchalantly, he jiggled his foot, looking for all the world as though he might begin humming contentedly at any moment.

As Georgie took the chair beside him, she felt a twinge of apprehension as she watched the petulant look on Greenwood's face turn to one of resignation.

"So what have you got for me today?" he asked Murdock.

With a slow, dangerous smile that Georgie was glad wasn't directed at her, Murdock considered the smaller man. "Well, you know, Greenwood, it's funny about that. Because for some reason, I was about to ask you the same thing."

Greenwood sat a little straighter in his chair. "What's that supposed to mean? Are you trying to tell me something?"

"Yes, I think I am." With a quickness that startled Georgie, Murdock suddenly leaned forward and thrust his face within inches of Greenwood's. "I think I'm trying to tell you that you're a liar. I'd also like you to know that if you don't start talking—and talking straight— you might just wake up tomorrow without all your parts in the right places. Am I making myself clear?"

Wide-eyed with shock, Georgie glanced nervously at the other customers in the bar, but no one seemed to be paying them the slightest attention. Anxiously, she leaned forward and laid a hand on Murdock's arm. A steely band of muscle jumped at her touch, but he didn't turn around.

Greenwood ran the tip of his tongue over his lips. "Yes, I think you've made yourself perfectly clear."

"Good. So let's have it."

Greenwood twisted in his seat. "Unfortunately, there's nothing I can tell you. I've already told you the—"

Before Georgie could blink, Murdock's hand snaked out and grabbed a fistful of the other man's shirt. "You think I'm fooling around? You think I don't mean business? You're going to tell me the truth this time, or so help me, I'll—"

"Umm, excuse me," Georgie said, softly clearing her voice. "Pardon me."

Murdock glared at her, still holding tight to Greenwood's shirt.

Georgie smiled primly. "Maybe if you let go of Mr. Greenwood and I explain a couple of things to him, we might all get along a whole lot better."

"What?" Murdock growled.

"What?" Greenwood echoed.

Leaning forward, Georgie slapped Murdock's hand. "Let go of him." She smiled at Greenwood. "Mr. Greenwood, I don't think you understand the urgency of our situation. Yours, too, I might add. You see, so far, at least three people who were connected to Jimmy Ray Thompson are dead."

At her words, Greenwood's face whitened and went slack. With a puzzled frown at Georgie, Murdock released the man's shirt.

"So you see," Georgie said pleasantly, "we're naturally concerned about your safety. Aren't we, Murdock?"

At her continued stare, Murdock finally shrugged. "Yeah, sure."

Georgie gave him a smile of fond approval. "Now, Mr. Greenwood, some parts of your story seem to be just a little bit made up. I'm sure you have a very good reason for that. But if you want us to help you, you're going to have to tell us the whole story now."

"Who were they?" Greenwood squeaked. "Who was killed?"

As Georgie took a breath to answer, she heard Murdock move restlessly beside her. She ignored him.

"Well, first there was another man who, like you, wanted Jimmy Ray watched. He was fished out of the river. Then Jimmy Ray's old cellmate from prison ended up looking like a pincushion. And of course, there was also the third jewel thief, who was stabbed to death just after the Meckelmann robbery."

At her last words, Greenwood went very still.

Georgie laid a hand over his clenched fingers. "That's what you've really been interested in, isn't it? The Meckelmann jewels."

Nervously, Greenwood glanced at Murdock.

"Is that why you wanted Jimmy Ray watched?" Georgie pressed him gently.

Greenwood gave her a scared look. Then slowly he nodded.

"Well, see? That wasn't so hard. Look," she said, turning to Murdock. "We're getting somewhere now."

Murdock merely grunted and slunk down in his chair.

"Now, Mr. Greenwood, can you tell us *why* you're interested in the jewels and Jimmy Ray?"

Greenwood shook his head.

"Oh. I see." Georgie frowned thoughtfully. "Well, you know, I think you're going to have to. Because if you don't, we just might start to think you're the third jewel thief." She smiled ruefully at him. "He's the only one unaccounted for, you see."

"Me?" Greenwood said tightly. "Oh, no. I'm not—" Falling back in his chair, the man looked from her to Murdock and back again. Closing his eyes, he sighed and reached inside his suit jacket.

Like a shot, Murdock leaned forward, tense and alert as Greenwood pulled out a small, white card and laid it on the table between them.

Picking up the card, Georgie read aloud, "Erskine Greenwood. Claims investigator. Northern Metropolitan Insurance."

Widening her eyes, she handed the card to Murdock.

"You're working for the insurance company," she said.

Greenwood nodded and eyed them anxiously. "I'm not supposed to let anyone know. But yes, that's my job."

"Not very good at it, are you?" Murdock grumbled.

"No. No, I suppose I'm not. That's why I hired you. For almost four years we've been looking for those jewels. They never turned up after the robbery, you know. And when Jimmy Ray Thompson was arrested, he insisted he didn't know their whereabouts. At the time, we believed him. We thought the third thief had somehow made off with them."

"But now you don't?" Georgie asked.

"No, now we don't. You see, it's standard practice after a theft of this size to try to trace the stolen property. Of course, we paid off the claim to the Meckelmann estate, but naturally we'd like to recoup our losses if at all possible. It was a, er, a rather heavy loss."

"But what changed your minds?" Georgie asked. "Why do you think Jimmy Ray knows where the jewels are now?"

Greenwood nodded at Murdock. "He'll tell you. It's apparent that Jimmy Ray is getting money from somewhere. Our guess is he has the jewels stashed somewhere, and now he's fencing them off one by one."

"And the third thief?"

Greenwood shrugged. "Maybe he's the one killing off all Jimmy Ray's acquaintances. He's got to be desperate to get those jewels back."

Georgie turned to Murdock, raised her eyebrows questioningly and shrugged.

"Have you ever heard of a man named Howard Kavin?" Murdock asked.

"Kavin. Kavin." Greenwood glanced away. "No, I don't think so. Is he important?"

Georgie's heart sank.

"No, he's not important," Murdock answered, avoiding Georgie's eyes.

Greenwood watched them, his dark eyes curious. "What are you going to do now that I've told you everything? Are you going to stay on the case?"

Murdock scowled without answering.

"It could be worth your while," Greenwood said. "If you find those jewels for us, there's a large reward. Over a quarter of a million."

Murdock's head snapped up. "Oh, really?" he said dryly. "Nice of you to finally get around to mentioning it."

The other man shrugged and gave them a thin-lipped smile. "You can't blame me for trying to save the company some money."

ALL THE WAY HOME, Georgie grinned with irrepressible glee. "My word," she said for the tenth time. "A quarter of a million dollars. Think of it, Murdock. We could be rich. I could pay off my school loans. I could buy the nicest, sweetest little nursery furniture. My word. A quarter of a million dollars."

"We haven't got it yet," Murdock reminded her as he pulled up to her apartment. "For starters, we haven't any idea where those jewels are. We aren't even sure if Jimmy Ray has them."

"No, you're right. We're not *positive*, but we have a pretty darned good idea."

Despite himself, Murdock let out a small, amused chuckle and shook his head at her. "You're pretty sure of yourself, aren't you?"

"Of us," she declared. "I'm sure of us. We'll find those jewels. And the man who killed Howard Kavin."

Murdock's smile faded. "Yeah. Him. Let's not forget about him. He's what I'd call a major hitch in the proceedings."

She stared out at the empty street. "Do you think Jimmy Ray killed Howard? And Walters?"

"I don't see how. We've been watching him practically around the clock."

She turned in her seat, her eyes troubled. "You said you thought Kavin was working for someone else, right? Well, if he was, then who was it? Who hired *him* to come to Poulopoulos Investigations to hire *me* to watch Jimmy Ray? It wasn't Greenwood. He already had you. It wasn't Jimmy Ray, because that's absurd. So who else is there?"

"The third thief," Murdock said. "The guy in the shadows."

She gazed out the window again, and Murdock saw her shiver. She wrapped her arms around herself.

"Look," he said awkwardly. "If the case is getting to be too much for you—"

"It's not too much for me," she said quickly. "I can handle it. It's just a little spooky, that's all. Not knowing who he is or what he looks like...or where he might be."

Some of her disquiet was rubbing off on him. Murdock felt a cold tingle down his spine, and suddenly he was afraid. He was desperately, urgently fearful—not for himself, but for her.

"Georgie, listen to me for a minute. I know you think you can handle things, and probably you can. But something about this case doesn't feel right to me. Maybe you'd better back off a little."

"Back off? Are you kidding? I can't do that."

"Just for one day. Tomorrow I'm going down to that hotel where Kavin was living and nose around a little. Then I thought I might do some backtracking on Jimmy Ray. Go over the old files, trace some of his old friends. Who knows, maybe I'll even turn up the name of the third thief."

She was staring at him, her eyes more wounded than angry. "And what am I supposed to do while you're out solving the case? Sit home and knit booties?"

His smile felt false, even to himself. "The kid's going to need them."

"Very funny."

"You're going to be a mother, Georgie. You're going to have a baby." Glancing down at her stomach, Murdock tentatively, almost timidly, reached out a hand. Then he quickly drew it back. "You want to be in one piece for that little guy, don't you?"

He wasn't sure if she noticed his move to touch her. Had she stiffened just the tiniest bit?

She sniffed. "It's a *she*. I hope. And no, I can't think of a worse thing to do to a kid."

Murdock gave her a look of genuine bewilderment.

"Oh, don't you see?" she cried, apparently exasperated beyond endurance at his stupidity. "I could stay home cowering, but what kind of an example would that be? If I march out there with my head held high, full of confidence and the belief that I can do it, then *that's* a good role model. *That's* the kind of mother I want my baby to have."

For a moment Murdock could only blink in astonishment at her. Gradually, a slow smile split his face.

"My God, you are one amazing woman," he finally said.

"I'm glad you finally noticed." Pushing open her door, she stepped out, then peered back into the car. "Do you want to come up?"

Murdock stared down at his hands, resting on the steering wheel. Did he want to come up? What kind of question was that? Of course he did. He wanted it with every fiber of his being.

Across the darkness, her eyes watched him. He shook his head. "I better go. Long day tomorrow."

He thought he saw her face fall. "Oh. Right. Okay, well, I guess I'll see you later."

"Georgie—"

Eagerly, her head popped back through the open door. "Yes?"

"I'll, umm, I'll give you a call tomorrow. Probably in the evening. Tell you what I found out."

"Oh." She nodded slowly. "Sure. I'll talk to you then."

"Good night," he called, but she had already slammed the door and was scurrying up the sidewalk.

For a long time he sat in front of her building, watching the lights in her apartment go on one by one. He told himself he was only sticking around to make sure she was okay. But when he'd sat there long enough to see the last light go out, he knew he'd only been fooling himself.

Yet he didn't go up to her. Instead, he started the Buick and slowly drove into the night.

9

"I'M SORRY, Georgie, but that's the way it's going to be. My decision's already made."

Georgie stood in the center of Nikos's office and wondered if she was going to be ill. Only, it wasn't morning sickness that had her stomach heaving this time. Clutching a small container of milk and a brown paper bag with her breakfast of three gooey donuts, she fought the sudden rush of nausea as the room tilted crazily around her. As though from a great distance, she heard the swish of morning traffic in the street below, the rattle and hiss of the radiator against the wall and the hard, staccato hammering of her own heart.

"You're joking," she said again.

Uncle Nikos shuffled a small sheaf of papers, tapping them on the desk to align the edges. He wouldn't meet her eyes.

"There's too much work in the office for Annie to handle all on her own anymore. The office is where you're needed." He smoothed the top page of the pile. "Of course, this won't affect your salary."

Georgie's throat tightened. "You're not even going to give me another chance?"

Nikos pretended to search in the top drawer of his desk. "I don't need another investigator. I need office help."

"But I'm not a secretary. I can't even type with more than three fingers. When you hired me, it was as a trainee. An *investigative* trainee."

"Things change."

"You mean, things heated up. Mom called you, didn't she?"

Nikos shut the drawer firmly. "My mind's made up."

"This is because of the family. You're going to knuckle under to them. You're going to let them—"

Nikos's head snapped up and his heavy face was set in stubbornness. "You should have told me you were pregnant. Now the whole family's after my butt. They're blaming *me*, and that doesn't make me happy. Even your grandmother called last night."

"Grandma called?"

"Cosmo is right. Detective work is no job for a woman whose about to be a mother."

"About to be a—" Georgie raised her arms, still holding her breakfast. "Do I look like I'm going to give birth at any moment? I can do the job. I can handle another case. You know I can. You can't listen to the family when you know darn well—"

Pointedly, Nikos picked up the pile of papers before him and looked at the first sheet. "The matter is closed."

"But—"

"Closed." He grabbed a pen, scrawled a signature at the bottom of the sheet, slapped it on the desk and turned to the next page.

Slowly lowering her arms to her sides, Georgie stared at her uncle. Gradually, her dismay gave way to a simmering anger.

All her life she'd been pressured and urged to be like her sisters, while she'd clawed and scratched to follow her dream. She'd fought hard and all alone to get through the criminal psychology program. Still, no one took her seriously. Even when she thought she was finally going to have an opportunity to prove she could be a detective, the chance was snatched from her.

But this time, Georgie thought, she wasn't going to give in.

"All right," she said. "If that's how you feel, then you leave me no choice."

Georgie raised her chin. "I quit."

THE PAVEMENT OUTSIDE Jimmy Ray's building was still dotted with puddles from last night's rain, and soggy leaves and litter clogged the gutters. Against the gray, overcast sky, the bare branches of the trees looked black and skeletal. Even the old buildings seemed to droop a little as though an air of weary desolation had settled over the whole street.

Despondently, Georgie leaned her head against the side window of her car and watched a stray dog nose among the black plastic bags of trash someone had set out at the mouth of an alley. Her eyes burned, her head ached from crying and a huge gaping hole seemed to have opened up inside her.

Her whole life, Georgie thought morosely, was going to hell. Pregnant, unemployed and alone—things couldn't possibly get any worse. Oh, what was she going to do?

With a loud sniffle, Georgie wiped her nose with a tissue and then sniffled again. If only she could find those jewels . . . If only Murdock would realize how much she loved him and . . .

But no, Georgie told herself firmly. She couldn't start fantasizing about "what ifs." She couldn't let herself begin to dream again. Look where all her dreams had gotten her so far. She was about as close to finding those jewels as she was to spotting the Loch Ness monster. She'd walked out on a job that she'd probably end up begging and pleading on her hands and knees to have back. And she was in love with a man who barely tolerated her, who couldn't bring himself to touch her and who was never ever going to return her love.

Cold despair, raw and biting, gnawed at her insides, and Georgie covered her mouth with her hand to hold back the fresh onslaught of tears that threatened to overwhelm her. With a protective gesture, she draped an arm over her belly. *Oh, little one*, she thought, *your mom has made a mess of everything. You poor, tiny tyke*.

Maybe everyone was right. Maybe she would never make a good detective, and she should just admit defeat. The odds against her just seemed too great to fight any longer. All these years she might have been following nothing but a pipe dream. Who was she to think that she could have something more—could *do* something more with her life?

Maybe it was time to stop trying so hard. She couldn't keep beating her head against the wall. After all, she had a child to consider now. Besides, in the end, what choice did she really have? No one was ever going to hire her as a P.I. And as for Murdock . . .

Murdock would be relieved when she was no longer in his hair.

The yawning hollow in the center of her chest opened a little wider, and Georgie swallowed hard against the despair. For once in her life, she told herself with forced confidence, she was going to be practical and levelheaded. She was going to do the sensible thing and give up her dream of being a detective.

She just wished that it didn't feel so awful.

With a last sniffle into the tissue, she sat up and reached for the ignition. It was time to go home, she told herself. It was time to give up and go home. Starting the car, she put it into reverse and raised her eyes to the rearview mirror.

It was then that she saw him. Jimmy Ray Thompson with his insolent, loose-limbed walk was moving down the street, swinging a jacket from his hand and glancing cautiously from side to side. Georgie froze, holding her breath, and watched him turn the corner, headed for the row of garages where he kept his Porsche.

She could feel a tiny pulse beat below her jaw, and her eyes were fixed on the now-empty street corner. With her hands gripping the steering wheel, she shook her head.

No, she thought. No, she was going home. She was giving up the battle. She wasn't a detective anymore.

Yet she sat there, breathless and immobile, and watched as the silver Porsche appeared. The sports car paused for a moment at the corner, then suddenly it turned left and headed down the street away from her.

With shaking hands and warring thoughts, Georgie pulled the Volkswagen out into the street and followed.

SLOUCHED BEHIND the wheel, Murdock steered the Buick with one hand and snarled at the evening rush-hour traffic around him. After hours of fruitlessly knocking on doors in the seedy neighborhood around Kavin's old hotel, he'd gone to the newspaper morgue and badgered the clerks there with about as much success. The only thing he'd learned of any value was that

Greenwood definitely worked for Northern Metropolitan Insurance. After a day of fishing, it wasn't much of a catch.

His feet hurt from pounding the pavement, his head throbbed from squinting at fuzzy microfilm and he couldn't seem to get the damp, decaying stench of the run-down hotel out of his nostrils. In fact, it would have been a completely wasted day if he hadn't decided at the last minute to stop by the station and ask for Orin Dobbs.

With his usual nonchalance, Dobbs had handed him his only new piece of information on the case, that the cops had long suspected that the third accomplice on the Meckelmann heist was a guy named Boyce McClury. After Murdock had grumbled his displeasure at not being told sooner and Dobbs had ribbed him about missing something *they* all considered common knowledge, he'd shown Murdock the McClury file.

The guy was definitely one of the nastier, meaner forms of life the city had ever spawned. His rap sheet read like an encyclopedia of felonious crime. The only problem was, McClury had disappeared around the time of the robbery and he hadn't bobbed to the surface once in all that time. If he'd been in on the heist, Dobbs told Murdock, then there was a good chance he'd gone the way of the other thief—the dead one.

Impatiently now, Murdock tapped his fingers against the steering wheel, laid a fist on his horn and swore a blue streak. At last the light changed and he made a right at the corner.

Maybe he should have felt satisfied with his day's work. After all, he *may* have dug up an important clue. But the truth was, after a long sleepless night of tossing and turning and driving himself crazy with thoughts of

Georgie, he'd gotten out of bed this morning with a headache the size of a New Year's hangover and the disposition of an enraged lion.

Pulling onto Jimmy Ray's street, Murdock muttered grumpily to himself. Reilly had probably deserted his watch hours ago. There would be no chance to dash home and shower or grab something to eat. He'd be stuck here in the damned Buick again all night without any coffee and only his thoughts to keep him company.

It was those thoughts that were the real aggravation. No matter what he did to try to stop them, thoughts of Georgie plagued him. The clear, bell-like music of her voice, the slow, seductive curl of her smile, the way her green eyes seemed illuminated from within, the softness of her skin under his hands—he couldn't escape his thoughts of her.

Everywhere he turned, he seemed to hear and see her, and it was starting to grate on his nerves. Somewhere in his gut he was beginning to realize the awful truth—that the more he saw her, the more this burning need for her seemed to smart and throb. And yet, seeing her was the only balm, the only salve that could cool the stinging ache. All in all, it was a hopeless—

With a puzzled growl, Murdock stopped the car almost directly opposite Jimmy Ray's building.

"What the hell?" he muttered, and craned forward to peer through the windshield.

In the middle of the street a block away, a small, skinny man in a ragged coat and floppy gray sneakers weaved back and forth on an ancient bicycle. Despite his erratic swerving, the cyclist was pedaling as fast as his short legs would go. In amazement, Murdock saw the man was Reilly.

"Boss! Boss!" Reilly shouted, and collapsed in a heap of limbs, spokes and dirty rags.

"Boss," Reilly repeated, frantically trying to free his coat and scarf from the handlebars. "The girl's gone."

Murdock glared at Reilly's struggling form. "What are you talking about? What girl? And where did you get that infernal contraption?"

"The girl in the red car. You said I was s'pose to keep my eyes peeled for her. Well, she was here."

Murdock's frown deepened. "How long ago? Which way did she go?"

"That's what I'm trying to tell you, boss. She took off after the guy. Man, that's some nice car that dude has."

Murdock felt his face blanch. "When did this happen? Where did they go?"

Tugging his coat free, Reilly scrambled to his feet and searched his pockets. "'Bout fifteen, twenty minutes ago. I followed 'em on my trusty steed here and— Ah, damn! Look at that! I broke my bottle." The little man gave Murdock a look of abject misery.

With suddenly cold hands, Murdock pulled out his wallet and thrust two twenties at Reilly. "Which way did they go?" he said between clenched teeth.

"That way." Reilly pointed down the street. Holding up the bills, he closed one eye and gazed greedily at them. "Thanks, boss. This'll go a long way to keeping my poor body—"

"But where, damn you? Where?"

"Huh? Oh, yeah. Not far. Just down to that old warehouse on Mulberry. The one with the—"

"I know the one. He's been there before. Did she follow him there?"

"Didn't I just say—"

Murdock felt the blood pound in his temples. "Damn it! Did he go in? Did she follow him in?"

"Yeah. That's what I been saying."

"Oh, my God . . ."

Without another word, Murdock put the car in gear, hit the accelerator and the Buick squealed down the street.

THE OLD WAREHOUSE was dark and musty. Most of the doors and windows had long ago been boarded over, and the only light came from the jagged holes made by vandals and two cracked skylights high overhead. Fear gripped Georgie's stomach like a fist of ice as she huddled behind a stack of rusty metal drums listening to the sound of her heart race. In the corner Jimmy Ray was grunting and cursing.

For the last ten minutes, she'd watched as he strained at one heavy concrete block after another. Her curiosity and dread grew as the pile grew smaller.

Peeping over the top of a drum, Georgie scanned the murky gloom, and saw Jimmy Ray's lanky figure bent over the last of the blocks. She bit her lip. What now? she asked herself. Unbelievably good luck had been dropped in her lap, but she could only juggle it like a hot potato.

He was going after the *jewels*. She knew he was. Under that pile of blocks was something he'd gone to a lot of trouble to hide. And that could only be the Meckelmann loot. But unless she came up with a brilliant idea—and came up with it quick—that knowledge wasn't going to do her a lick of good.

With increasing panic, Georgie watched as Jimmy Ray heaved the last block to the side and straightened. He stretched his back and wiped his hands down his spindly jean-clad legs. Kneeling, he began to pry up a section of the concrete floor with a small crowbar.

Georgie gnawed the tip of her thumb. In desperation, she searched the shadows of the warehouse. She heard a grunt of satisfaction. Jimmy Ray had shifted the slab, and he reached in to pull out a small bundle wrapped in plastic.

As she watched, he fumbled with the package, stripped the plastic away and held a small, white canvas bag to the light. Georgie's heart thudded as his head turned toward the metal drums. Quickly she ducked down, and her fingers closed over an egg-sized chunk of broken concrete.

When Jimmy Ray rose to his feet, Georgie said a silent prayer. Closing her eyes, she threw the concrete as hard as she could.

From the far side of the warehouse, she heard a loud clank, then a muted thud. From the sudden curse he gave, Jimmy Ray heard it, too. Georgie peered over the drum and nearly wept with relief. Jimmy Ray had frozen in alarm. Carefully, he set the bag on the ground and began to slink quietly toward the sound.

Georgie's heart thudded and her knees grew weak. Yet, when Jimmy Ray stopped halfway across the warehouse, she suddenly leaped from her hiding place, surprising even herself with her panicked speed.

Nearly sobbing with terror, she scrambled over the broken floor and was nearly at the bag when she heard him shout.

"Hey! You!"

Without coming to a complete stop, Georgie swooped past the bag, her fingers closing around the neck of the little sack as she flew by. She heard his footsteps, loud and pounding behind her. With a tiny gasp of horror she glanced over her shoulder, saw his furious face in the dim light and stumbled over a metal pole.

She scrambled to her feet and raced for the dark opening of a hallway with Jimmy Ray fast on her heels.

"You bitch! Stop! My God, I'll kill you."

Georgie cried aloud and scurried down the hall, clutching the bag to her chest. At the end of the hall a steep flight of metal stairs ran up into the darkness of the warehouse. Wild with fear, Georgie stumbled up them.

She was nearly at the top when she felt his hand close over her foot.

"No!" she screamed, and kicked out at him.

He gave a muffled curse and released her, but her relief was short-lived. The stairs opened onto a perilously decrepit metal catwalk. Beneath her feet she could see the concrete floor far below, and with her first step the whole structure swayed and shuddered.

Jimmy Ray reached the top of the stairs, his hollow-cheeked face twisted with fury. Terrified, Georgie stared back at him, unable to tear her gaze from his. With the bag clasped against her, she took a backward step down the catwalk.

An ominous creak echoed high in the warehouse ceiling, and the catwalk quivered and shook under her feet. Very slowly, Jimmy Ray smiled, a horrible smile of cruelty.

"Give me the bag, bitch," he said. "Or I'm coming out there to take it from you."

Dry-mouthed, Georgie took another faltering step backward. The catwalk screeched as metal tore on metal.

Jimmy Ray's eyes narrowed, and his smile twisted. "Too bad," he said as he stepped onto the catwalk, "you won't live to regret this."

From somewhere in the darkness below, a voice bellowed, "Georgie! No!"

The next instant a tremendous blast rent the air. In a whirling, dizzying moment of horror, she saw Jimmy Ray jerk spasmodically. His eyes met hers in surprised bewilderment. Then he was gone, toppling over the edge of the catwalk to the floor below.

Georgie screamed shrilly and slumped to her knees. Through the grill walkway, she could make out Jimmy Ray's broken body beneath her, his legs bent grotesquely. She screamed again and buried her face in the dusty canvas of the bag.

Footsteps thundered up the iron steps. A gruff, familiar voice shouted at her. When she looked up, Murdock stood teetering on the brink of the catwalk.

"Georgie," he said quietly. "Come on back now. Can you make it back?"

Dazed with shock, she stared at him. "Murdock?"

"It's me. I'm here. I'm right here. But I can't come out to get you. This thing won't take my weight. And it isn't going to last much longer. You've got to crawl back here, Georgie. Do you hear me? You've got to do it now."

"Oh, Murdock. Jimmy Ray... Oh, my God."

A foreboding shriek of ripping metal shattered the quiet.

"Come on, Georgie. You've got to come *now*."

With wide, staring eyes she took in his face, the rough planes and angles made harder still by tension. She began to inch forward, pushing the bag ahead of her and never taking her gaze from his face.

When she was still a yard from him, she felt the cat-walk tremble and heard a slow, high-pitched grating that quickly grew louder. In that moment of paralyzing fear, she saw him rush forward. Strong hands gripped her arms, nearly yanking them from her shoulders, just as the catwalk fell away beneath her. For the briefest of moments she felt her legs dangle in mid-air, and then she was pressed against his wide chest.

"Georgie," he groaned into her hair. "You little *idiot*."

"The jewels! The jewels!" she cried over the roar of crashing metal and stone. Dust rose into the air, making them cough.

Murdock gazed down at her, then slowly raised his hand. He held the little bag. "Is this what you're looking for?"

"Oh, Murdock. Jimmy Ray... I can't believe—" She broke off and smiled up at him. "You saved my life."

"Well, I—"

"You did. He was going to kill me. He said he was. And you shot him."

She felt Murdock stiffen and pull back from her, his face astonished. "Shot him?"

"Yes, and you saved—" At the expression on his face, Georgie stared at him.

"My God," he breathed. "You're right. That *was* a gunshot I heard as I was coming up the stairs. We heard the report."

"But I don't understand. Didn't you—"

"It wasn't me. I didn't shoot Jimmy Ray," Murdock said slowly. "I never fired my gun."

At his words Georgie's breath caught, and an icy coldness moved across her skin. "Then who . . .?"

Together they turned and looked down at the twisted metal and billowing dust that covered Jimmy Ray's body.

SHE SAT cross-legged on his bed and watched him with wide, uneasy eyes as he paced the length of the one-room apartment.

When he'd half carried her out of the warehouse and piled her into his car, he'd driven home in stony, ominous silence, too shaken to notice that he'd brought her back to Eddie's until they were already sitting in front of the tavern. Without a word he'd marched her past an astonished Eddie and several gaping customers, who exchanged long, significant looks when he ignored their greetings and herded her straight back to the hall.

Glancing at her now, he suddenly realized why he'd never invited another person to this place. Even coated with dust, she looked so bright and fresh and alive that the room looked even more drab and gray in comparison.

"My God," he burst out unexpectedly, stopping in the center of the room. "This case is getting out of hand. You could have been killed back there."

"Well, I wasn't," she said emphatically. Less certainly, she added, "But Jimmy Ray was. Oh, Murdock. What are we going to do? Good heavens, what are we going to tell Sergeant Dobbs?"

"Dobbs. Good God. Dobbs." Running a hand roughly through his hair, Murdock stopped and stared at the ceiling. "We're not going to tell him anything. Not yet, anyway."

"But we can't just leave Jimmy Ray there. Not like that."

"I'll make an anonymous call. But we aren't going to tell the cops anything. Not until we figure out this mess."

"Who . . . who do you think it was?"

"I don't know, Georgie. I just don't know. My God, he must have come into the warehouse just after me. I didn't see anyone outside." He looked a little ill. "Unless he was down there, waiting for you."

"But who could it have been?"

Murdock wheeled on the thin, colorless carpet and began pacing again. Thoughtfully, almost to himself, he said, "Could it be? It *has* to be. Boyce McClury must have finally decided to show up again."

"Who?"

He explained what he'd learned from Dobbs that afternoon. When he finished, she sat back and stated, "It had to be this man. He sounds exactly like the type. And you said he's already killed before."

"A number of times."

"Oh, Murdock! The third robber, Howard, Walters and now Jimmy Ray! This man's on a killing spree. We've got to find him."

"I don't think that's going to be too hard." Murdock indicated the pile of brilliant, glittering diamonds and sapphires, pearls and emeralds that spilled across the worn bedspread beside her. "He seems to have a knack for finding anyone connected with the jewels, all by himself."

"You think he's going to come after us."

"I don't think we're going to give him a chance. I'm going to see Greenwood right away. I'll tell him we have the jewels and arrange a swap. The sooner the better."

"A swap?"

"The reward money, Georgie."

"Oh, yes." Her solemn face brightened. "I nearly forgot about that. It almost seems wrong to think about the reward right now. I mean, after everything."

"We earned that money. Especially you."

She looked a little proud. "Yes, I did, didn't I?"

"Don't get too cocky. We haven't got it yet."

"Before we go, I want to wash up a little first. Is that all right?"

He blinked at her. "You aren't coming with me, Georgie."

"What?"

"You heard me. You're hiding out here until I get everything arranged. I don't want you out there where anyone can take a potshot at you. Besides, someone has to stay with the jewels."

"Then *you* stay."

"You're not coming with me."

"But that's not fair. If it wasn't for me—"

"You almost *died*, Georgie. Jimmy Ray was going to kill you. You could have been shot."

Her forehead creased in a frown, and she glanced up at him. "Yes, but . . . *I* got the jewels."

"The jewels?" he hollered. "What good are the jewels if you're dead? Huh?"

As he watched, her face crumpled a little, and her eyes darkened with hurt. "I did the best I could," she murmured softly.

Something in her look stabbed him to his soul, and he ran a hand roughly through his hair.

"Oh, God," he said, and dropped to the bed beside her. Lifting a hand, he raised it to her cheek, hesitated for just an instant, then touched her dirty, tear-streaked face. "You look like a street urchin."

Then suddenly his arms were around her and he crushed her against him, burying his face in her hair. He shuddered at the thought of how close she'd come to death—how close he'd come to losing her—and his embrace tightened.

From against his shirtfront, a muffled voice asked, "Does this mean you like me again?"

Pulling away from her, he held her at arm's length and narrowed his eyes.

"You're a pain in the neck," he said.

She watched him soundlessly.

"You're no good for me, Georgie."

Still her eyes watched him.

"I'm no good for you," he insisted.

Her dark hair was tangled and mussed, a smudge of dirt was smeared across her nose and a small piece of tar paper had gotten stuck to her cheek. Yet, when her lips parted in a smile, he thought she was the most beautiful woman he'd ever seen.

"So, you kind of like me then," she said.

He knew he should turn away. He knew he should jump to his feet and march out of the room. Go tell Greenwood his jewels were safe and end it all right there. He knew that was what he should do. And yet, he couldn't tear his gaze from hers.

"Yeah," he said brusquely. "I like you. I like you too much, Georgie. I like you so much it scares the hell out of me."

Her eyes grew troubled, and she tilted her head quizzically. "But why? Why should that scare you? Because of the baby? Do you not want to—"

"For God's sake, Georgie. I can't explain. It just won't work. You've got to forget about it. I can't! I can't . . . love you."

He heard the bed squeak as she moved beside him. A slim arm settled protectively over his shoulders.

"Is she your daughter?" Georgie asked softly. "The little girl in the picture."

The breath left his body in a painful rush, and he went rigid under her touch.

"Is that why you won't even try? Does it have something to do with her?"

When his breath returned, it burned his lungs like fire. His voice sounded like a low echoing rumble from deep within a well. "Don't talk about her."

"But why? She looks like a sweet little girl. Surely she wants you to—"

"She's dead."

In disbelief he heard his voice, ragged and hoarse, say the awful words. The fire in his lungs seemed to blaze up, erupting in his head like a whirling explosion of black anguish. Flinging off her arm, he jumped to his feet. With clenched fists he stood in the center of the room and struggled to keep himself from falling into the fiery, black pit.

"I'm sorry," he heard her say, her voice raw with distress.

He closed his eyes. "I'm going now," he said carefully, willing his voice to remain empty and flat. "I'll be back by ten."

Seizing his hat and coat from the chair, he headed across the room. At the door he paused and, without turning back, added quietly, "Don't open the door to anyone."

GEORGIE SAT for a long time on the bed, holding the photograph. The woman was beautiful, dark and exotic like a strange, tropical flower. The little girl had her mother's black eyes, but her hair was wheat-colored and her face was square and sculpted like her father's.

At nine o'clock she replaced the picture on the mirror, scooped the jewels back into the bag and took a long, hot shower. She found a blue shirt on a chair by the door. Raising it to her face, she drank in the warm scent of him, swallowed hard to suppress a sob and pulled on the shirt before turning off the cracked table lamp. Lying between the sheets on his bed, wrapped in his shirt, he seemed to surround her—to fill her senses with his smell. His presence. Turning on her side, Georgie stared at the photograph on the mirror.

She had nearly dropped off to sleep when a sound brought her fully, alertly awake. Wide-eyed she gazed into the darkness, listening intently. Just as she decided her nerves were playing tricks with her, she heard the creaking sound again.

Rolling over in bed, she stared at the window. Through the dingy curtains, she could see the colorful lights from the tavern windows below and could just make out the dark shape of a telephone pole several yards outside the window.

Frowning, she pulled herself up in bed and threw off the sheet. But before she could swing her legs out, a small gasp escaped her lips. There against the pane was the unmistakable outline of a gloved hand.

10

THE FIRST THING Murdock saw as he drove home from his meeting with a grateful and relieved Erskine Greenwood was the blue flashing lights. Cops, he thought. Not an unusual sight in this neighborhood.

Only when he turned onto his street did he realize just how many police cars were needed to create the kind of blue, flickering glow he'd been able to see even from several blocks away. Half a dozen of them were parked every which way, scattered crazily across the street as though they'd descended on Eddie's from all directions.

Cold terror seeped into Murdock's bones. His heart faltered, and his breath... He couldn't seem to catch his breath. My God, he thought in a wild frenzy of fear. My God, Georgie. Georgie.

Squealing to a stop, he threw open his door and was out of the Buick before it had even settled. A noisy, curious crowd was gathered outside the ring of police cars. He forced his way through them, shoving blindly as he ran for the tavern.

"Hey, wait! You can't go in there, buddy."

With a furious growl, Murdock shook off the cop. Another blue uniform stepped into his path. Too panicked to bother sidestepping the man, Murdock barreled ahead and simply ran over him.

"Hey, stop that guy!" he heard behind him as he stumbled into the deserted tavern and pounded down the hall for the stairs.

Cops swarmed everywhere. In the darkness, the tiny apartment seemed filled to capacity with large, heavy-shouldered men. Standing in the doorway with his hands gripping the frame for support, Murdock stared in horror at the scene. His breath was hoarse and ragged, and his whole body seemed to have turned to ice.

My God, he thought wildly. It was his fault. It was all his fault. He'd left her alone. He'd been so upset, he hadn't thought of anyone but himself. He'd left her all alone and unprotected.

"What's this guy doing up here, Frank?" one of the cops asked, turning to Murdock.

As the man stepped back, Murdock saw what had been previously shielded from his view. A pair of legs, stretched out on the floor, the body hidden by the plainclothes cop that knelt over it.

A groan of anguish erupted from Murdock's throat, and he clutched the door frame to keep from sinking to the floor. A hand touched his arm, and he jerked back.

"Murdock," Orin Dobbs said. "Are you all right? You look like hell, man."

"Murdock?" a small, light voice piped up. "Is that you, Murdock?"

In disbelief Murdock scanned the shadowy room. A large officer in a camel overcoat looked down at someone, then stepped backward, letting a small figure with wild dark hair pass by him.

"Nice job, lady," the policeman said, and patted Georgie's shoulder.

Dazed and suddenly weak with sickness, Murdock gaped at her as she strode through the gathering of police, all of them pausing to smile at her and offer warm congratulations. She was beaming, grinning from ear to ear and accepting their praise with little humility. She looked like the cat that ate the canary.

She also was wearing nothing but one of his blue shirts.

Slowly, the numbing horror began to seep away, only to be replaced by relieved anger and mind-boggling confusion. Murdock turned to a smiling Orin Dobbs, then back to Georgie. He looked at the man sprawled in the center of the room and who, even as Murdock watched, began to move his head, shaking it in lazy befuddlement.

"What in God's name is going on here?" The question burst from him in a loud bellow.

Several of the cops turned to glare at him.

"Oh, Murdock!" Georgie cried, and ran up to him to throw her arms around his waist and lay her head against his chest. "I'm so glad you're back. I was never so scared in my whole life."

Still dull with shock, Murdock hesitantly laid a hand on her back and patted it awkwardly. He could feel Dobbs's eyes on him.

"That's some, er, assistant you got there," Dobbs said, his voice full of laughter. "She'll probably get a commendation from the mayor."

"I will?" Her head popped up.

"I wouldn't be surprised. Single-handedly capturing a wanted fugitive. I'd say that deserves a medal."

"Wait a minute. Wait just a damned minute," Murdock barked. "What fugitive? Who is that guy? And what's he doing in my apartment?"

"It's Boyce McClury," Dobbs said.

"He tried to break in," Georgie chirped in. "I hit him."

"You *what?*" Murdock gripped her shoulders.

"Over the head. With your table lamp." She grimaced. "Oh, yeah. I'm sorry about your lamp."

Several cops hauled McClury to his feet. The man held his head groggily, staggering so weakly they didn't even bother to handcuff him. Dobbs stepped aside to let them pass. Dry-mouthed, Murdock watched them lead McClury out the door.

"My guess is he saw you leave," Dobbs was saying. "He thought he had an open field. Man, he must have been one surprised dude when Georgie here whacked him over the head."

"He *was* surprised," Georgie said brightly. "He said 'Oh, shoot' when I hit him the second time and then he just sort of fell over."

"'Oh, *shoot*'?" Dobbs questioned, laughing.

"Well, something like that."

"The thing is, I think we've got Howard Kavin's murderer," Dobbs said.

Murdock's head snapped up.

"Yeah. She convinced me about that one." Dobbs looked pleasantly rueful. "Anyway, my bet is that McClury's been waiting all these years for Jimmy Ray to get out of the slammer. When he did, McClury saw his chance to recover the jewels."

"He was the one who hired Kavin," Georgie offered. "It was him all along."

"Yes," Dobbs said. "He's admitted that, although I'm sure he'll deny it when he comes to his senses. And of course, he denies killing Kavin. Denies killing Walters and Jimmy Ray, too. But what else is the creep going to say?"

At Murdock's strangled groan, Dobbs smiled again. "Oh, yeah. About Jimmy Ray. Georgie already told me all about your little fiasco with him and the jewels this evening. I've got a couple of men over at that warehouse right now. It looks like McClury saw his chance tonight and blasted Jimmy Ray while Georgie had him occupied. He probably would have tried to get the jewels back then, but you must have scared him away, Murdock. You two have been awfully damned busy lately, haven't you?"

"You told him about the jewels?" Murdock said tightly, giving her shoulders a little shake.

"Well, yes. I had to. How else could I explain why McClury was lying here unconscious?"

"But why did you—" Murdock scowled at her as he took in her attire. "And why the hell are you dressed like that? You're walking around half-naked with all these guys around? Where are your clothes?"

She gave him a funny little frown and pointed over her shoulder. "Over there."

"Well, what—why," he stammered. "Isn't that my shirt? Why are you . . . ?" Glancing sharply at Dobbs, who was grinning, Murdock's scowl grew heavier. "It's not what you're thinking."

Dobbs shrugged and raised his hands. "I wasn't thinking anything, old buddy. It's none of my business how you treat your employees."

"She's *not* my—"

"I was sleepy."

Dobbs's grin broadened. "See? She was sleepy."

"Oh, for the love of—" Murdock broke off. "She's still not my employee. Do you hear, Georgie? You aren't my assistant."

Dobbs turned to her. "But I thought you said you got fired today and were working for Murdock now."

"Well, I didn't actually get—"

"You got *fired*?" Murdock thrust a hand into his hair. "When did this happen? Why didn't you tell me? You didn't tell *me* you got fired."

"You never gave me a chance. And anyway, I didn't really get—"

Dobbs hooked his thumbs in his belt loops. "I don't think you're going to have much to worry about, at any rate. Not now, anyway. Not with the size of the reward the insurance company's going to give you for recovering those jewels." He moved away to join the cluster of policeman by the window.

Murdock groaned aloud. "You told him about *that*, too."

She made a face. "I guess I did. It just must have slipped out with everything else."

"Great. Just great."

From the corner of his eye, Murdock saw one of the cops give Georgie a long, appreciative look, his gaze lingering on her bare legs. Snarling under his breath, Murdock strode to the bed, ripped off the sheet, and sent the man a black, dangerous look. Without a word he wrapped the sheet around her.

"Are you almost done in here?" he barked.

Dobbs turned and gave him a significant wink. "Don't worry. We're almost finished. You two can be alone in a minute."

"Damn it, Georgie," Murdock muttered. "I can't leave you for a second."

BY THE TIME Dobbs and his men finished photographing, examining and fingerprinting, Georgie was curled next to Murdock in the big, red chair, fast asleep.

"Looks like she's all done in," Dobbs said, buttoning his coat.

Murdock grumbled incomprehensibly.

"She's quite a woman," Dobbs said thoughtfully. He caught Murdock's eye. "It's about time you finally settled down. If you ask me, you couldn't have picked any better."

Murdock looked away. "Well, I didn't ask you, did I?"

Dobbs shook his head sadly. "Just give her a chance, buddy. That's all. Just a chance."

Murdock gazed darkly at the far wall. After a few seconds he heard Dobbs move away and close the door behind him. Nuzzled against him, her legs drawn up under her, Georgie murmured sleepily. Very gently he ran a finger down her smooth cheek, brushing back wispy tendrils of hair from her face.

He should wake her. He should tell her to get dressed and go home. But he couldn't find it in his heart to send her away. Did she know how frightened he'd been? Did she know his anger was nothing more than a reaction to his overwhelming fear?

Because he *had* been afraid, more afraid than he'd been in a very long time. For a short while tonight, he had thought he was living the nightmare all over again. For a brief instant he'd known that losing her would be as devastating and as damning as the loss of Kristen.

He wasn't sure he could stand it. He wasn't sure if he could bear to lose her. And *that* more than anything else terrified him.

In her sleep she smiled softly and snuggled closer to his side. A rush of tenderness swelled in him and he bent to kiss the top of her head, drinking in the clean, soapy scent of her hair. She was so lovely. Dobbs was right. He couldn't have picked a finer woman. But he hadn't picked her. At one time, he hadn't wanted anything to do with her.

Now, with her nestled in his arms, he knew that wasn't true any longer. He wanted her. He wanted her now and tomorrow and forever. But could he take the chance again? This time—oh, dear God—*this* time, would anything be any different? Would she grow to hate him? If he looked into her eyes one day and saw only disdain, he knew it would kill him.

And what about the baby? Didn't her child deserve something better than what he could give? If he walked away now, there would be a chance for her. She would find someone else, and her child would have a father who didn't make the kinds of mistakes *he* had made.

Once more she stirred in her sleep as though his very thoughts were capable of disturbing her. She yawned, and a slow, sad smile touched his lips.

"Georgie?"

"Umm."

With an aching heart, he clenched his jaw and said, "You have to get up now. You have to go home."

"Umm. Don't want to."

"You have to."

"So tired. Let me sleep."

"You can't sleep here."

Her eyelids fluttered, and she looked drowsily up at him. She smiled softly. "You keep me warm."

"No. No, you've got to go."

She wrapped her arms around his neck, burying her face in his shirt. "Going back to sleep."

"Georgie."

"Good night."

He gazed down at her tangled hair, at the arch of her back as she curled against him, and he swallowed hard.

"Georgie, damn it. You can't stay here. Don't you understand? If you stay here, I'm going to make love to you again. And I can't do that."

She moved her face against his chest. When she looked at him, some of the sleepiness had gone from her green eyes. "Yes, you can. I want you to."

Oh, good God, he groaned inwardly, staring down at her soft, parted lips, at the tiny pulse that beat at the base of her throat, and at the dark, seductive hollow between the open buttons of his blue shirt. Despite himself, his heartbeat quickened, and he felt the blood in his veins run a little hotter.

"Georgie, I don't—"

"I want to stay with you."

His mouth went dry. He wanted to protest, but instead he lowered his head and covered her lips with his.

Cradling her cheek in his palm, he skimmed his fingers down her slender throat to caress the hollow at the base of her neck and stroke the silky skin between the open buttons of her shirt. Raising his head, he watched his hand in fascination, loving the sight of his own hard, rough fingers on the soft white skin of her breast.

When he looked up, her green eyes had grown stormy and dark. Turning in his arms, he felt her fingers lightly brush his whiskered cheek.

"Do you always get your own way?" he asked huskily.

"No." She smiled lazily. "But I'm working on it."

"You're becoming pretty good at it. With me, at any rate."

Her green eyes danced. "Am I?"

"Oh, yes," he murmured, trailing his fingers down to the buttons on her shirt. "It must be all the practice you've been getting lately."

Slowly, tantalizingly, he undid the buttons and gently pushed back the shirt. His gaze roamed her body, drinking her in. Sitting up, she helped him slip the shirt off her shoulders.

"My God," he said roughly. "I can't seem to help myself around you. I can't seem to get enough of you."

"Then why try?"

Cupping one upturned breast in his hand, the sudden touch of her soft skin in his rough palm made his body harden and tense. Why try? she'd asked him. He knew the answer to that question. There was a reason, a damned good reason. But somehow, at this particular moment, it didn't matter. Nothing else mattered but the warm silkiness of her skin under his hands.

He reached for her, slipping a hand under her legs and pulling her against him. Sighing with pleasure, she curled in his arms and let him carry her to the bed.

When he stripped off his clothes and leaned over her, she raised her arms to him—inviting him, welcoming him, enticing him to her. Lying beside her, he drew her close, groaning at the satiny coolness of her skin against his. His lips found hers, and he pulled her closer still.

He could feel his desire, hard and throbbing like a hunger in his gut. His lips left her mouth and trailed down her throat. Wrapping her arms around him, she clung to his shoulders as his tongue circled her breast and his lips nuzzled a taut nipple.

He gently laid a hand on her stomach, spreading his fingers wide across her slightly rounded belly.

"What about—" He broke off. "Is this okay? For the baby, I mean."

Her eyes were wide and dazed with desire, and it took her a moment to register his words. When she did, he saw her smile.

"Of course it's all right. The baby's fine."

"You're sure?"

A puzzled look crossed her eyes. "Yes. But I thought—"

He stopped her words with his kiss. Sliding his hand down her belly to her most private part, he heard her give a tiny gasp of pleasure. She was warm and wet and he wanted her so badly his senses reeled with the need.

"Murdock," she moaned, her face buried in his shoulder. "I need you, Murdock. I love you so much."

Those words, murmured in the heat of passion, meant nothing, he told himself. Yet, they brought him up a little short. Raising his head, he gazed down at her. Her eyes, dark green with longing, held his.

"I love you," she repeated more strongly.

He closed his eyes and turned his face into the dark, lustrous mass of her hair. *She loved him*, he thought as fear and elation pounded through him. My God, she loved him.

And suddenly the fear was gone, and there was only Georgie. Georgie with her arms twined around his neck. Georgie arching up, offering herself to him. And he would take her. He would take her and hold her and never let her go.

Raising himself, he settled over her, parting her legs with his thigh. Her eyes searched his, and though he couldn't bring himself to say the words that hovered on his tongue, when he bent his head and covered her mouth with his, he put all the desire and love he couldn't express into that kiss.

His body ached for her, and when she moved her hips impatiently against him, he could stand the anticipation no longer. Gently, he eased inside her.

With a groan of delight he slowly filled her, his eyes never leaving hers. His breath quickened and his chest heaved, and she moved with him, wrapping her legs around him to bring him closer still.

"Georgie," he moaned, his hips moving with hers.

She loved him, she loved him, she loved him, his heart beat out rhythmically, faster and faster. The aching hunger in him swelled, and then suddenly he was crying out her name. The whole world splintered, falling into blackness around him, and as it shattered he held on to the one thing he was suddenly sure of.

She loved him.

AT TWO-THIRTY that morning, Georgie sat cross-legged on Murdock's bed, licking her fingers. Beside her, Murdock was stretched out, large and muscular and completely naked. His head rested back against a pillow, and he was smiling at her.

"Are you sure you don't want another piece? You only had two."

"Hmm," he answered, his smile widening. "Do all pregnant women eat like you do?"

Lifting a slice of cheesy pizza from the cardboard box, Georgie paused. "I don't know. I expect they do. Unless they're having morning sickness. I've got both."

"Both?"

"Uh-huh." She took a bite and chewed blissfully. "Half the time, the thought of food makes my stomach turn. The other half, I'm famished."

"That's crazy."

"I know." She shot him a bright smile. "Well, *you* should know that."

The second the words left her mouth, she regretted them. The smile faded from his face, and it felt as though a cold wind had just blown into the room. Georgie laid the pizza down, suddenly not very hungry anymore.

"I'm sorry. I . . . I shouldn't have said—"

"No," he said forcefully, sitting up. "No. Don't be sorry. You haven't said anything wrong. It's true that I should know. But I don't. I wasn't around very much back then."

Georgie realized her mouth was open, and she quickly closed it. He was looking across the room, yet she didn't think he saw anything there. He seemed to be staring beyond the room, at something very far away that only he could see.

"I was a lousy husband, a worse father, and my wife left me. It was a long time ago."

Shoving the pizza box to the end of the bed, Georgie crawled over to him and laid her head on his chest. She could hear the hard, solid beat of his heart and feel the tickle of his chest hairs against her cheek.

She felt him pat her shoulder tentatively as if afraid to touch her. Then suddenly he lay his hand full on her back. When he began to speak, his hand tensed, then relaxed, over and over.

As though the words had been dammed up inside him, they came out in a breathless, furious rush, and Georgie had to close her eyes against the pain in his voice. He told her the whole story, and all the time she felt his hand clenching and unclenching against her back.

"You see," he finally said, "I had to make a choice. Yet no matter what I chose, I was damned forever. For one brief moment I wanted to kill Isabel for what she'd done. If I had, I would have carried that around with me like a curse for the rest of my life. But because I didn't, I lost my daughter. If I had known that Kristen was going to die that night, would it have made any difference? Would I have risked my soul—eternal damnation, if you believe in that stuff—to save my daughter?"

"But you didn't know," Georgie said, rising to her knees. "You couldn't have known. At that moment you did the right thing. You let her walk away. The accident wasn't your fault."

"Wasn't it?"

There was something terrible in his eyes, a hopeless, haunted weariness.

"No," Georgie said vehemently. "No, it *wasn't* your fault."

"If I had been a better husband, a better father, none of it would have happened."

"And if I hadn't been stupid enough to sleep with Stuart the Rat Lice, I wouldn't have this miraculous little baby growing in me right now. Oh, Murdock. There are some things in life you can't control. You can't do anything about fate. It just happens. It's nobody's fault."

He gave her a skeptical, uncertain look.

Leaning toward him, she took his hard, weathered face in her hands and kissed him.

"I love you," she said. "It doesn't *really* make sense. I don't *really* know why. But I love you so much it feels sometimes like it's burning me up. You can't explain that, Murdock. You can't plan or prevent or change that. It's fate. I love you, and I don't know why or how. I just know I always will . . . as much as you love me."

He frowned. "I never said—"

"Oh, yes, you did. You said it tonight."

"I did?"

She nodded, smiling. "You tell me all the time."

"I do?"

"Yes. It's something I'm just beginning to realize. You just don't exactly use words."

"I don't get it."

"I know," she said with a smile, and laid her head down on his chest again. "But you will."

11

SITTING ON THE EDGE of the tub with a cool washcloth pressed against her forehead, Georgie breathed deeply, willing the last of the nausea to leave her.

"Georgie?" For the tenth time, Murdock called through the bathroom door, his voice as worried as the first time. "Are you sure you're all right? Can I get you anything?"

"No," she mumbled. "I'm fine."

"You don't sound fine."

"I'll *be* fine."

She could hear him breathing heavily on the other side of the door. He rattled the knob. "How do you know this is normal? Maybe you ate too much pizza last night or maybe . . . maybe something's wrong."

Georgie reached over and unlocked the door. He must have been leaning against it because he suddenly stumbled into the bathroom, filling it with his large presence. He clutched a shirt in one hand, and his bare chest was ridged with muscles, with a small patch of dark, curly hair that disappeared in a thin line into the waist of his jeans. He looked a little startled.

"Nothing's wrong," she stated firmly. "I've got morning sickness. That's all it is."

"How do you know?" he asked, his gaze sweeping over her anxiously. "I think we should get a professional opinion. I'll call Greenwood and tell him we'll meet him some other time. We'll go back to that doctor, the one you saw—"

"Murdock! I'm not going to see the doctor. There's nothing wrong with me. We're going to meet Greenwood and get that reward money."

"Well then, I'll go alone. There's no reason for you to come, too. You stay here and rest. You need to take it easy. You need your energy to—"

"Oh, for crying out loud, if you don't stop bugging me, I swear I'm going to scream."

He frowned at her and ran a hand through his hair fretfully. "Maybe the last few days were too much for you. A woman in your condition shouldn't be running through warehouses and hitting felons over the head and—"

"Murdock, listen to me." Leaning over, she put a hand on his leg, unable to suppress a small, tender smile of amusement. "I'm not dying. I'm pregnant. It's not a terminal illness. Women have been doing this since time began. There's nothing to worry about."

He balled his shirt in his hands. "I'm not worried. I'm just . . . concerned."

"It's only a baby," she said kindly.

"I know that. But it's, well, it's not normal."

"Not for you." Her smile widened. "You're a man. But my body's built for this. It can handle it."

He'd crunched his shirt into a small wad. Doubtfully, he eyed her, then nodded sharply twice. "Yeah. Yeah, okay. You're right." He moved toward the door, started to put on the shirt, then paused uncertainly. "You're sure?"

"Positive. Oh, and Murdock?"

He spun back. "Yeah? What is it?"

"Maybe you'd better find another shirt to wear."

"Huh?" Glancing down, he smoothed a hand down the damp and crumpled shirt. "You think so?"

"Definitely." She gave him an encouraging smile.

"Yeah, okay. Maybe you're right."

When he'd gone, Georgie shoved the bathroom door shut. Burying her face in the washcloth, she burst into gales of smothered laughter.

THE OFFICE of the insurance company was a small shed of corrugated steel about the size of a mobile home. This far out from the main terminals of O'Hare Airport, the landscape was a flat desert of runways, empty as far as the eye could see.

As Murdock parked the Buick a short distance from the office, a jet thundered overhead, its engines kicking up a stiff wind and renting the air with their blast.

"I can't believe this is really happening. My first case, Murdock. Oh, think of that reward!" Beside him, Georgie was practically bouncing on the seat in excitement, her high spirits having steadily increased with every mile they'd driven. "Look, that must be the plane the money came in on."

A small private jet sat halfway between the office and a cluster of hangars.

Georgie grinned at him. "This is so much more fun than a boring certified check. I'm so glad you made him pay us in cash. In just a few minutes we'll be able to run our fingers through lovely green bills."

Murdock smiled and flicked an escaped strand of hair from her cheek. He'd had wanted to conduct their transaction at the bank, but Greenwood thought it would be a little safer to meet at the plane. When he'd explained, a little dryly, that transporting jewels and large sums of money around was how the whole mess had started in the first place, Murdock had finally agreed.

"I think I see him now," Murdock said, watching a small dot far down the road grow rapidly larger. "He's a little late."

"You don't think something went wrong, do you? Maybe he'll insist on an expert taking a look at the jewels."

"Greenwood *is* an expert. He's also been working on this case for four years. He knows these jewels like the back of his hand. He also knows we won't try anything funny. We've got too much to lose."

Georgie sighed and smiled. "Boy, I can't wait to see the look on Uncle Nikos's face when I tell him. He's going to kick himself. And my family is going to be so surprised. Of course, they aren't going to like it any better, but at least they won't be able to say I'll never make a good detective."

Leaning over, Murdock took her face in his hands and gave her a loud, resounding kiss. "You *are* a good detective. Turned out a lot better than I'd thought. In fact, I've been thinking about—"

A large, black sedan pulled up near them in a shower of gravel. Automatically, Murdock patted his leather jacket, feeling the heavy, reassuring weight of his gun. They watched breathlessly as the driver's door opened and Greenwood climbed out. He carried a small leather suitcase and a hanging bag.

"Sorry I'm late," he shouted over the roof of his car. "I had some trouble with my hotel bill. Did you bring them?"

Opening his door, Murdock turned to Georgie. "You stay here. Let me deal with this."

"But I don't want to—"

His eyes held hers. "Please," he said quietly.

In surprise, she slowly nodded.

Murdock let out a deep sigh and reached for the canvas bag at her feet. "I'll be right back."

Unexpectedly, a shiver of apprehension coursed through her, and Georgie reached for his hand. "Make him show you the money."

He smiled back at her. "Of course."

"And be careful."

He gave an odd, bemused shake of his head and stepped onto the tarmac. From where she sat, Georgie could see the whole length of Greenwood's car and the man standing patiently by the hood. Murdock joined him.

The two men seemed to discuss something, and a moment later Greenwood walked away and across the tarmac to the plane. Murdock turned back to her and winked.

Greenwood reappeared carrying a black briefcase. The wind blew the sides of his suit jacket back and tossed his thin, carefully arranged hair, revealing a pink bald spot. When he reached the black car, he set the briefcase on the hood and opened it.

Georgie saw Murdock smile and bow his head to examine the contents. Then she watched in stunned disbelief as Greenwood raised his hand. As though the world stilled into slow motion, she saw the gun barrel meet the back of Murdock's head. He jerked in surprise, then clutched at the hood as if to steady himself. A silent scream tore from her throat when he crumpled to the ground in front of the car.

She was out of the car and running for him before she knew what she was doing.

"Stay back!" she heard Greenwood scream. "Stay back!"

His words meant nothing to her. Unable to stop, driven by wild and raging fear, she fell on her knees beside Murdock. In horror she stared at the blood that matted his thick, golden hair.

"Stay back, damn you. Or I'll shoot," Greenwood hissed. "I swear to God, I'll shoot you down."

Raising her face in numb anguish, she stared blindly up at Greenwood and the gun he pointed at her.

"It was you," she whispered hollowly. "You. All the time."

His cold eyes narrowed, and his thin lips spread in an arrogant, malevolent smile. "I've waited four years for these jewels, and if I have to kill you, too, I'll gladly do it. So get down. Face on the ground."

Georgie stared at him, paralyzed by grief, unable to breathe.

"On your face, I said!"

As though something vital suddenly snapped in her, Georgie heard the furious snarl that rose from deep inside her. In a blinding blur, she hurled herself forward, tackling Greenwood around his waist and grabbing for the hand that held the gun. He was not a large man, and under the impact he staggered in surprise.

"Stupid bitch!" he shrieked, and brought the gun toward her head.

Then suddenly they were both falling, tumbling across the tarmac. She hit the ground and rolled several feet away, the breath knocked from her lungs. A growl more vicious than Georgie's erupted in the air around them, and in a flurry of flying fists, she saw Murdock kneeling on Greenwood's chest, pounding at his head.

From where she lay sprawled and gasping on the concrete runway, Georgie struggled to catch her breath. "No!" she finally screamed. "Murdock, no! Stop! For the love of God, stop hitting him!"

In an agony of pain and nausea, she curled her knees up to her chest. "Stop," she whimpered once more.

As if her voice had finally gotten through to him, Murdock suddenly went still. She could hear Greenwood moaning and then heard Murdock's voice telling her to get the handcuffs from his car.

His voice seemed to fade in and out, and sweat drenched her face. With an effort, she tried to sit up, then fell back.

"I can't," she gasped.

Murdock looked over at her sharply. Almost without glancing down at Greenwood, he gave the man's temple a stunning blow that made him go silent, then scrambled to his feet.

"Georgie," he cried, running his hands over her. "What's wrong? Georgie! What's happened?"

"Hurts," she panted. "Murdock. My stomach. Hurts."

"Oh, my God."

Bounding to his feet, he stared wildly around the open tarmac, then dropped to his knees beside her. "I'm going to go call for help. I'm going to the office. Don't worry about *him*. He'll be out for a while. He won't bother you now. But I'll have to leave you for a minute."

With tiny jerks of her head, she nodded and squeezed her eyes against the red-hot pain stabbing through her. "The baby," she wailed.

With a shaking hand, he brushed her hair back from her face. "It's going to be fine, sweetheart. It's going to be all right."

And then he was gone. With a quiet moan of pain, Georgie rested her cheek against the rough concrete and wept.

MURDOCK SAT in the plastic chair, his head bowed. He felt as if he'd been staring at the same white square of tile between his boots for a million years. In the hall outside the waiting room, footsteps approached and he raised his head, only to see the white figure of a nurse bustle past the doorway.

Across the room, a row of dark, hostile eyes watched him. With a tremor of despair, he bowed his head again.

"I'm going to get some coffee," one of Georgie's older sisters said. "Does anyone want some?"

He heard the murmured answers of her family, then felt a light tap on his shoulder. He roused himself and glanced up.

Her sister peered unsmilingly down at him. "Coffee?"

"Uh, no. No, thanks."

She shrugged and moved away, and once again he felt the eyes burning into him, accusing him. Yet no one could despise him more than he despised himself, Murdock knew. How could he ever have let her come along with him? She'd saved his life, throwing herself on Greenwood that way. And yet he'd give that life a hundred times if only she would be okay.

The squeak of crepe-soled shoes entering the waiting room caused a tense rustling as they all sat up, anxious and alert. With a collective sigh of weariness, they settled once more as Orin Dobbs nodded politely at the Poulopouloses.

He settled himself on a small plastic chair beside Murdock. "How is she?" he asked.

Murdock shook his head, unable to answer. Raising his fist to his mouth, he gnawed at his knuckles.

"Well, I thought you'd like to know that we've got him. He confessed everything. Kavin, Walters, Jimmy Ray—he did 'em all. Man, that is one sick individual you handed us. He thinks the Meckelmann jewels are his. I don't know. He's been planning this whole thing for four years. I guess he handed so many fortunes back to the insurance company, he thought they owed him one."

Murdock nodded, barely listening.

Dobbs shook his head. "It was a pretty sweet plan for a lunatic to come up with. All he had to do was tell the company the investigation was a washout, then quietly retire with the jewels...and the reward money. That he had to rub out three people to get to those jewels doesn't seem to have bothered him a bit. Keeps looking at us like we're crazy and telling us not to worry about the murders because they were all criminals anyway. Geez."

"Mr. Murdock?" a voice said.

Dull-eyed and numb, Murdock turned his head, then sprang to his feet. He stared at the white-jacketed doctor, his mouth going dry.

"Your wife's going to be fine, Mr. Murdock."

With a muffled groan, Murdock sank back into his chair. A babble of laughter and cheers rang around him as Georgie's family hugged one another in relief.

"She's a strong, healthy young woman, and I see no reason why she shouldn't make a full recovery," the doctor went on. "We had a few bad moments there. That was a pretty bad fall she took. But I think we're out of the woods now. You can see her if you want."

Across the room, Murdock's eyes met Cosmo Poulopoulos's. For a moment, the two men gazed at each other in shared trepidation. Then Cosmo nodded at him and asked gruffly, "And the baby? Did she lose the baby?"

The doctor smiled. "Oh, no. The baby's fine. She's not far enough along for a fall to do much damage."

Murdock closed his eyes and muttered a silent thank-you.

"Of course," the doctor added loudly, holding up his hand to try to quiet the sudden outbreak of voices, "of course, she's going to have to take it easy for a while. She'll need someone to look after her for a few weeks at least."

"She'll be coming home with us, she will," Maggie Poulopoulos stated quickly.

Murdock took a deep breath. "No," he said. "She has me. I'll take care of her."

Maggie's shoulders stiffened and her green eyes flashed—just, Murdock thought, like another pair of green eyes.

"She's my wife," Murdock said, waving at the doctor. "Or will be. You heard him."

"She'll *not* be going with the likes of—"

Beaming merrily, Cosmo laid an arm over his wife's rigid shoulders. "Now, Maggie, you heard the boy. Don't be an interfering mother-in-law before we even have the wedding."

"But he's the one who brought all this terrible trouble on her, to begin with—"

"*And* he'll get her out of it." Taking a step forward, Cosmo slapped Murdock on the back and grinned at the doctor. "He's going to be my new son-in-law. Fine-looking boy, isn't he?"

The doctor gave them a bewildered look, and from somewhere behind him, Murdock heard Dobbs snort with laughter.

He couldn't have cared less.

FOR A MOMENT when he first opened the door, Murdock's gut went cold with fear. Lying in the hospital bed with ominous beeping machines around her and her face pale and peaked, Georgie looked so tiny and frail that he knew the doctor must have made a horrible mistake.

Then she turned her head and saw him, and the smile that broke across her face made his heart melt.

"Hi, there," she said quietly, pointing at the closed curtains around her.

His legs felt heavy as he crossed to the bed, but his soul was light. "How do you feel?"

"Like I ate too much pizza." She smiled tenderly. "How's your head?"

Reaching for her hand, he pressed it against his chest. "Oh, Georgie. I'm sorry. I'm so sorry about—"

"Ssh. Don't. Everything's okay now, Murdock. Everything's going to be just fine."

"But you were nearly killed."

His hand felt large and rough and protective around hers. With a little tug, she drew him closer.

"Nearly isn't good enough," Georgie said. "I'm a better detective than that, you know."

When he finally smiled back, she nearly sighed aloud with relief. She'd been so afraid—so frightened that he would use what had happened against himself and would retreat still further away from her. Maybe, just maybe, he was going to take the chance, after all.

"Can I ask you something?" she whispered.

"Sure. Anything."

"Why do all the doctors and nurses think I'm your wife?"

He pulled back a little, his face reddening. He gave her a rueful look. "Well, kind of because of your name, Georgie. I mean, I couldn't spell it. Hell, I can't even pronounce it. So I told them you were Georgie Murdock."

Georgie blinked. "You did?"

"I think it sounds better, anyway. In fact, I think you should probably keep it that way." He gave her an anxious, hopeful look. "Don't you?"

For a long stunned moment, Georgie gaped at him. "Are you . . . are you asking me, um, what I think you are?"

"I think I am."

A silly smile played on her lips. "Oh, boy."

His gray eyes grew even more serious and worried. "Well?"

Georgie studied him in silence, then crooked her finger at him. "First, I want to know something."

He leaned closer, his face stiff and tense.

"What is your first name?"

At her question, his jaw hardened and his eyes shifted away from hers. Indecision and chagrin crossed his face. Then very slowly he bent his head, put his lips to her ear and whispered.

Georgie pulled back against the pillow and stared. "No, it isn't."

He nodded dolefully.

A burst of laughter escaped from her lips. "Really?"

"I'm afraid so. And now that you know, I can't let you get away, can I? I *have* to marry you."

With a squeal of laughter, Georgie lifted her arms to him. "I guess you really do."

When his lips touched hers, it wasn't bells they heard but applause. From behind the curtains that ranged around them came loud, enthusiastic clapping, although none as ardent as the ovation of Georgie's entire family huddled in the open door.

Once more Murdock's eyes met hers. They smiled at each other. With surprising ease, they forgot about everyone else in that next kiss.

Over the sound of cheering, one thin, elderly voice asked querulously from behind the nearest curtain, "But what was his name? I didn't hear. What was his name?"

Epilogue

PAST A WIDE, gleaming marble hall with a fountain and miniature jungle of potted greenery, across to a bank of glass-enclosed elevators, up the elevators to the sixteenth floor and down a wide hallway of thick, gray carpet were double glass doors under the bronze-sculpted letters of a sign reading Murdock and Murdock, Ltd., Private Investigators.

Inside the suite of offices, a phone was ringing, and a receptionist answered, twisting her earring as she talked. Across the waiting room in a large, expansive office with a sweeping view of the Chicago skyline and two enormous desks, Georgie fiddled with a pencil, frowned at a report and quickly dashed several more notes across the typed page.

She glanced at her watch and sighed. "I've got to go meet Westheimer in fifteen minutes. Do you think he'll mind if I just read this report to him? I scrawled all over it."

Behind his own desk, Murdock stretched in his chair, his boots resting on the edge of the desk. With one finger, he raised the brim of the hat that covered his face.

"Huh?" he asked wearily.

Georgie set down her pencil and smiled at him. "I told you that you didn't have to do double duty. You were out on surveillance all day yesterday and the night before on the Darrens case. I could have taken your shift."

"You do your own shifts. Leave mine alone."

"We could call that nanny service."

"Not on your life." Lowering his hat, he folded his hands over his broad chest and sighed. "It does feel good to put my feet—"

A wail, thin and plaintive, drifted in from the small annex room next door. Murdock sighed, sat up and pushed his hat to the back of his head.

"I'll go," Georgie said, rising with him.

"No, you have to meet Westheimer. The reputation of this firm depends on it," he said lightly and crossed the room.

Perched on the edge of the desk, Georgie felt a rush of tenderness so exquisite it was almost painful. Striding back into the office, Murdock carried a small, pajama-clad body against his huge chest. A tiny fist reached up and grabbed the brim of his hat.

"Cut it out, squirt," he said, his rough voice somehow gentle. "You'll have to get your own hat. This one's mine." Grinning at Georgie, Murdock patted the baby's back.

"Did you see?" he asked her. "I told you he wants a hat. I'm going to stop by that store tonight on the way home."

Georgie grinned and shook her head. "It'll rub off all his hair."

"It will?" Holding the baby up, Murdock gave him a long, serious look. "Did you hear that, Murdock? She thinks it'll rub off all your hair. In my opinion, there's not enough of it yet to take the risk. What d'ya say?"

The baby gurgled and punched him in the face with a slobbery little fist.

"All right." Murdock crossed to her desk, sat beside her and balanced the baby on his leg. "We'll hold off on the hat."

Leaning her head against his shoulder, Georgie laughed quietly and reached for the baby's tiny fist. "You know," she said. "I'm not sure it sounds right to call a four-month-old baby by his last name. Couldn't we call him—"

"Wait! No. Don't say it." Murdock gaped at her, then grinned. "He's Murdock. Just like his old man. Aren't you, buddy?"

Snapping her briefcase shut, Georgie laughed. "All right. But just until kindergarten."

"You're going now?"

"Yes, I've got to run. I think this could be it. If I'm right, the case could break tonight."

Murdock wiped the drool from the baby's chin with a large finger. "Here, here, Murdock. What's this? Got to keep up appearances, eh? So, did you catch all that? Mom's got a meeting. You know what that means. It's poker and cigars for us tonight."

As Georgie passed, Murdock reached out and wrapped an arm around her waist, drawing her close. "You'll be careful tonight?"

"Always."

"You'll call if there's any trouble?"

"I promise."

"Have I told you I love you?"

"In the past hour? No, I don't think so."

Pulling her still closer, Murdock rubbed his cheek against hers. "I love you, Georgie. I love you more than anything in the world. You've given me back my life, you know."

Standing on tiptoe, Georgie kissed his forehead, his cheek, then his lips. Nuzzling closer and tingling in all the places his fingers touched, she closed her eyes. "Oh, I love you, too."

"That's nice," he murmured against her mouth as his hand slipped inside her jacket. "But would you mind telling tell me just one thing, my darling wife?"

"Umm," she said dreamily.

"Why are you packing a gun?"

MILLION DOLLAR SWEEPSTAKES

SWP-M96

BRIDE'S BAY RESORT

UNLOCK THE DOOR TO GREAT ROMANCE AT BRIDE'S BAY RESORT

Join Harlequin's new across-the-lines series, set in an exclusive hotel on an island off the coast of South Carolina.

Seven of your favorite authors will bring you exciting stories about fascinating heroes and heroines discovering love at Bride's Bay Resort.

Look for these fabulous stories coming to a store near you beginning in January 1996.

Harlequin American Romance #613 in January
Matchmaking Baby by Cathy Gillen Thacker

Harlequin Presents #1794 in February
Indiscretions by Robyn Donald

Harlequin Intrigue #362 in March
Love and Lies by Dawn Stewardson

Harlequin Romance #3404 in April
Make Believe Engagement by Day Leclaire

Harlequin Temptation #588 in May
Stranger in the Night by Roseanne Williams

Harlequin Superromance #695 in June
Married to a Stranger by Connie Bennett

Harlequin Historicals #324 in July
Dulcie's Gift by Ruth Langan

Visit Bride's Bay Resort each month wherever Harlequin books are sold.

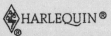

HARLEQUIN ®

You're About to Become a
Privileged Woman

Reap the rewards of fabulous free gifts and
benefits with proofs-of-purchase from
Harlequin and Silhouette books

Pages & Privileges™

It's our way of thanking you for
buying our books at your
favorite retail stores.

PROOF OF PURCHASE
Offer expires October 31, 1996
HT-PP152

Pages & Privileges ™

**Harlequin and Silhouette—
the most privileged readers in the world!**

For more information about Harlequin and
Silhouette's PAGES & PRIVILEGES program call the
Pages & Privileges Benefits Desk: 1-503-794-2499

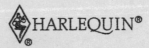

HARLEQUIN®

HT-PP152